I0666919

Undaunted

No Rival, #2

Charity Parkerson

--Warning: This book is intended for readers over the age of 18.

Editor: Vicky Reese
Cover art by Dar Albert
Originally published by Ellora's Cave Publishing under the
same title.
ISBN-10: 1-946099-02-3
ISBN-13: 978-1-946099-02-0

Introduction

No Rival Book 2

Brothers Rhys and Knox have been in love with the same woman for years. While Rhys has been open about his feelings toward Mandy, he's kept her firmly locked in the friend zone. That is, until a night filled with too much alcohol explodes into passion.

Unfortunately, Rhys doesn't remember anything of their hot night together. It's only when he encounters a passionate scene between two of his fight-buddies that Rhys recalls his night with Mandy and vows to make it up to her.
Mandy is tired of the drama. As secrets unravel her friendship with Rhys, Knox steps in to pick up the broken pieces of her heart.

Mandy must decide who to choose—the charming reprobate she desires, but who always wrecks her life, or the merciless bad boy who wants to give her the world.

Dedication

I need to send huge thanks and lots of hugs to Sarah Kurchak from Fightland for answering my questions even when they were a step beyond uncomfortable.

Chapter One

March

The crazed look in Rhys' eyes scared the hell out of Mandy. In all the years she'd known him, she'd never seen him come unglued. Blood streaked the white walls of his living room and several family photos hung broken inside their frames. Four new holes in the drywall would greet him when some of the alcohol left his system, but she imagined he wouldn't care.

She wanted to fix it. Sweat glistened on the flat pads of his chest and a bead rolled down his torso. She followed its progress over the ripple of his abs. An unwanted and badly timed burst of lust had her feet moving before her mind had time to catch up. Even as her fingers fanned his cheek, she knew it was a mistake. When his sweet brown eyes focused on her, it was too late to back down. His gaze never left hers even as he turned his head and pressed his lips against the inside of her wrist.

She craved him. It had always been Rhys and no one else. He would destroy her, and she was going to let him.

* * * * *

July

One. Two. Kick. Three. Four. Knee. Five. Six. Back kick. Rhys repeated the count in his head as he ran through his drills. It was a mindless act after all these years, but it was still necessary and part of the routine at the club. To say No Rival was an exclusive fight club would be the same as claiming Mount Everest was just another hill. As far as Rhys was concerned, there wasn't a higher honor for a

Vegas fighter than getting accepted into the private training facilities. Anyone who hoped to compete at a professional level drooled at the thought of sparring alongside the reigning heavyweight champion, Drew Alexander.

Rhys' membership was understood. Fighters were a family and fighting professionally ran in his. At one time, his father had been the middleweight champion, and everyone automatically assumed his three sons would follow, but Rhys wasn't happy to merely have the torch passed on to him. He wanted everyone to know he deserved to be there.

Only when his lungs burned did he snag the bag and hold it in place. Dragging a deep breath in through his nose, he caught sight of Drew watching him from the open doorway of the front office. The severe look lining the man's face wasn't unusual, but it seemed harsher than normal. He was almost always silent, but Rhys knew it was a side effect of a calculating mind. Everything from his large form down to the way he stood was part of his weaponry. Drew was deadly and it was why he'd never been beaten.

Rhys dipped his chin and Drew motioned him over. "Can I speak with you privately?"

With a nod, Rhys followed him inside the small room. Curiosity ate at his gut since Drew Alexander wasn't one to talk, whether it be privately or not. He couldn't imagine what could drive him to do so now. "I need a favor," he added as he closed the door behind them. Rhys was near to dancing in place with his need to know. If speaking to anyone was an oddity, then asking for favors was the equivalent of being struck by lightning.

"What can I do for you?" Rhys wanted to pat himself on the back when he managed to keep the interest out of his voice.

Acting as if he'd not said a word, Drew leaned against the desk and crossed his feet at the ankles. Bracing his palms on the wooden surface at his sides, Drew tapped his thumbs nervously until Rhys was ready to crawl out of his skin.

Just when Rhys thought he'd snap from the tension, Drew let out a heavy sigh and crossed his arms over his chest. "My father passed away last night."

It was on the tip of Rhys' tongue to say he didn't know Drew had a father. Luckily, some form of suck-ass condolences popped out instead and saved him from sounding like a prick. "I'm sorry to hear that."

Drew waved it away. "We only spoke

a couple of times, so he may as well have been a stranger. The thing is, I've been asked to do some honorary shit at the funeral, and I don't feel as if I can say no." Rhys grunted his assent, wondering what any of this had to do with him. Drew scrubbed at his scalp. "There's no way I'll be able to go without Aubree, but there's no fucking chance I am leaving her alone for one second while I'm there. So, you see my problem?"

Nodding, Rhys said, "No."

Drew barked out a laugh, and his eyes lit up, changing his entire face. It was odd. Rhys couldn't remember ever seeing the man smile. He'd never noticed the loss before now. "I'm in a real shitty position here, man," Drew admitted. "Most people don't know it, but I have a brother. To make a long story short, he once got a bit physical with Aubree when she wouldn't do something he wanted. I need someone to stay with her while I do my part. If you'd be willing to take the job, I'd like to hire you to work as sort of her private security for the day."

Rhys was stunned, and he wasn't even sure by which part. He didn't know Aubree well, but like everyone else in the MMA world, he'd known her father. When she'd married Drew he'd wanted to get to know her, but Drew turned out to have a jealous side Rhys would have never expected. He couldn't imagine anyone physically harming the sweet little blonde woman who'd snagged the world's deadliest man and living to tell about it. "This guy put his hands on her and is still walking around?"

"Yeah, about that," Drew said uncomfortably. "He almost wasn't. Walking around, that is," Drew clarified. He blew out a sigh. "I'm placing a lot of trust in you here. Seriously, I'm handing you enough shit to ruin me, but there is another reason I need you there. When I found out what happened, I flipped out and almost killed him. Honestly, I wasn't a hundred percent sure he would live afterward, and now with Aubree pregnant, this overprotective side of me is even worse. If he makes any attempt at all to speak to her while we're there, I'm not sure how I'll react. I need someone to keep me in check. I might kill him for real this time."

Rhys snorted before he could stop it. "And you think I could stop you if you decided to snap his neck?" To his surprise, Drew nodded.

"You have a better chance than anyone."

"Wouldn't one of my brothers be a better choice? I'm sure both Dane and

Knox would be honored to help. I'm not saying no. I'm only making sure." Rhys wanted to help, but he was equally aware he was the pup of the family. Even at six foot two, he was smaller than both of his brothers.

Drew hesitated, as if choosing his words carefully before answering. "Can I be honest?"

"Of course," Rhys answered immediately.

"We both know why I won't ask Dane, and you possess an empathy Knox doesn't have. Seriously, he probably knows someone who can make my brother disappear for me. In spite of my anger toward Max, I do understand he's lost his father and I know you will take his grieving into consideration."

Rhys couldn't argue with Drew's logic. A huge part of him wanted to defend his brothers, but he couldn't force himself to lie. Dane was a fucked-up mess and it was likely Knox more than knew someone who could make a person disappear. He probably was that someone.

"The pay would be good," Drew tacked on when he was too slow in responding.

Rhys didn't hesitate. "There's no need for you to pay me anything."

"I'd feel better if you let me."

"Nah. This is what friends do for each other. If the roles were reversed you'd do the same for me." Rhys wasn't sure it was true, but he knew Drew was a good man and wouldn't allow any woman to come to harm.

"You might not feel the same after I say this. Aubree can't know why you're there." Rhys groaned, and Drew nodded his understanding as he explained. "My brother Max was at one time someone she considered a good friend and Aubree has a loyalty streak a mile wide. She won't thank me for this."

"Ah, life on the edge. It keeps me from taking up too much space," Rhys deadpanned.

* * * * *

Mandy squared her shoulders as she left the kitchen area and headed for the crowded dining room. It was only her heart, she reminded herself for the thousandth time as she moved to serve yet another meal to one of Rhys' dates. She would survive another night of this. Circling the table, Mandy set a basket of dinner rolls down before moving to refill their drinks.

The girl was shooting daggers at her. Mandy could feel the murderous stare biting into her skin. With an inner sigh,

Mandy poured more water into her glass before moving to Rhys' side of the table. She wondered if should spit in the overly large-breasted woman's food and hope it caused her to develop some crazy strand of new disease. Maybe it would make her boobs slip to her ass. Mandy smiled evilly at the thought.

"Okay. Now, I have to know what you're thinking."

"What?" Mandy asked, attempting to keep the guilt from her voice even though she knew Rhys had known her too long to believe the false tone.

"You had this whole naughty thing going on with your face, and I have to know." She could feel the blades sharpening at her back, but Mandy kept her gaze locked on Rhys. "I have no idea what you mean." Rhys allowed her blatant lie to slide, and seizing her chance, Mandy added, "I have a business opportunity for you when you have a little time to talk it over."

Rhys waved toward the empty chair at his side. "I always have time for you. Have a seat."

The loud huff behind her made Mandy cringe and she really didn't want to talk it over while he was on a date. "You're a little busy right now."

"Actually, I'm not."

The huff turned into a horrible gasp. Mandy pasted on her best fake smile, speaking through clenched teeth. "All the same."

A lazy smile grew across his face, causing Mandy to wonder if she should sit down after all. In case her knees gave out. Rhys was ridiculous perfection. It wasn't fair to the rest of the world. Why did he come here and torment her, she wondered for the thousandth time. Her gaze slipped from his short-cropped brown hair to the cleft in his chin, and the memory of his lips touching hers caused time to slow as she continued staring at him.

"Excuse me, server, I'd like to eat before my food gets any colder. You should move along and do your job." Rhys' date threw enough venom behind the statement that a lesser woman would have run for the hills. The reminder of her presence hit Mandy harder than a truck. She was torn over who she was the angriest with. In the end, it was herself.

*

Rhys cringed inside at Crystal's nasty tone, and the look on Mandy's face made him wonder if he would get to see a good catfight. Saving Mandy from losing her job, Rhys cut off Mandy's retort. "What time do you get off tonight? Maybe I can meet up with you then."

Mandy's face brightened as she checked her watch. "I'm off at nine, so I only have around an hour left."

"He'll be…busy at nine," Ms. Snark said, reminding them both she was the one who was there with Rhys while making her intentions for the night clear.

"No. I won't," Rhys said, holding Mandy's stare as he added, "I'll be at your place by nine fifteen." This date had been a stupid idea, one he hoped might stir some jealousy in the stubborn woman holding his gaze, but he'd be damned if he'd allow Crystal to ruin any chance he had to spend time alone with Mandy.

Mandy was the first to look away and a small smile played on her lips. "I see Knox is here as well." She nodded across the room, but Rhys didn't bother looking in that direction. He saw Knox all the time and Black River was a popular place, so it wasn't surprising.

"Nine fifteen," he reminded her, awaiting her agreement.

She gave him a bland smile. "Sure. I'll go say hi, and let the two of you enjoy your dinner." With a final glance at their table, she walked away, leaving them alone.

Crystal had seemed like the perfect choice. Short, brown-haired and stacked, she was the polar opposite of Mandy. He felt absolutely no attraction to her. It wasn't her fault. She was a beautiful woman, but she wasn't Mandy. Now he couldn't wait for their date to be over.

By the time he finally managed to get Crystal home, things had only gone from bad to worse. She made several blatant attempts to lure him inside. At first, he made every effort to let her down easy.

It didn't work. In the end, he'd given in. He'd not even taken off his shoes. In and out in under fifteen minutes.

Crystal had been pissed that he was still leaving, there was no doubt about it. Not that he cared. Maybe one of these days he'd get his shit together and try to find a woman who could replace his fantasy of Mandy, but he doubted anyone could truly take her place. They'd been friends too long, but his body refused to turn down a beautiful woman, especially when she began to pout.

He beat Mandy home. Instead of waiting outside as he should, he flipped the flowerpot over and grabbed the spare key. After unlocking the door, Rhys tucked the key back in its hiding spot before he headed inside.

She'd left her kitchen light on again even though she'd bitch when her electric bill came in. He was glad for it since he hated her coming home so late by herself every night. Of course, as a prizefighter, Mandy's dad had ensured all his kids knew how to defend themselves, but Rhys preferred she not have a reason to use the knowledge.

Her tan walls and maroon couch felt like home to Rhys. He wasted no time kicking off his shoes and falling across the couch. He made a halfhearted attempt to find the remote to the TV before giving up and staring at the ceiling.

The fight scene was a small world, almost like family. When Rhys' father had secured him a membership with No Rival and began training him to compete, Mandy had been the first person he'd met close to his age. At seventeen, he'd already been too sure of his ability to win anyone he wanted. The moment he had her alone, he attempted to steal a kiss. He'd limped for two weeks afterward, but he'd been hooked. Since then, he'd spent as much time with her as he could get away with. His dad and brothers accepted her constant presence without question. The possibility they might not end up together had never really occurred to him. It was only a matter of time before he figured out how to convince her to keep him.

His mind swirled with possibilities when he thought of Mandy's business proposition, but he couldn't come up with a single thing that sounded probable. Two job offers in one day—he was a hot commodity. A flash caught him off guard and blinded him for a moment. Mandy's laugh rang through his ears. "Ha! Caught you." Damn, it was rare for anyone to get the drop on him. "Oh, that's a good one," Mandy said, staring at the digital screen of her camera.

"Let me see."

Mandy pushed away his wiggling fingers. "No way! You'll delete it." He couldn't argue with her logic. "Give me a second to change, and I'll be right back."

Mandy slipped into her bedroom while Rhys went back to staring at the ceiling. It did no good for him to think of her pulling off her shirt on the other side of the door. No more than a thin layer of wood stood between him and heaven, if he didn't count her absolute disinterest. Lack of willingness on her part did nothing to deter Rhys' idiotic need to possess her. It seemed nothing ever would.

Staying true to her word, Mandy re-appeared only minutes later wearing a baggy t-shirt, a pair of super-short cut-offs and nothing else. The long legs he'd pictured wrapped around his hips a thousand times taunted him now as he watched Mandy moving toward him. Not until his eyes met hers did he realize how long he'd focused on the lower half of her body. An odd expression, one Rhys couldn't decipher, crossed over Mandy's face. It disappeared before he had time to figure out what she was thinking.

Rhys opened his arms and without hesitation, Mandy crawled on top of him until she was snuggled down tightly between him and the couch. There was never an awkward moment of silence between them. Things simply were what they were.

With her cheek resting on his chest, Rhys could only see the top of her head when he spoke. "Guess what happened to me today?"

Mandy shifted until her leg was across his stomach and Rhys bit back a moan at the contact. Her lack of a bra and close proximity were taking a toll on him. "How many guesses do I get?"

"None. I got invited to a funeral," he said, too excited to share his gossip to wait on her to run through the possibilities.

"A funeral? I didn't realize people needed invites. I must know," she added in a teasing tone and he goosed her side.

"Behave or I won't tell you the good bits," he warned and she pretended to zip her lips. "Good girl. Drew's dad died and he's asked me to join him to keep an eye on Aubree while he's doing some honorary stuff."

Mandy nodded against his chest. "Ah, he's keeping her away from Max. That makes sense."

Rhys titled his head to the side. "You know about Max?"

He felt her shrug. "I don't know if I

know 'about' his brother, but I did meet him once at one of Drew's holiday parties. Of course, I didn't find out until later it was his brother I'd met. Actually, that's how Drew and Aubree met as well. She came with Max to the party."

"Huh," Rhys grunted. "A mystery. I will have some entertainment while I'm there, it seems."

His mind wandered off as he pictured a thousand different scenarios in which Aubree ended up assaulted by Max. Nothing he envisioned made any sense. His muscles relaxed and his eyes grew heavy as Mandy's warmth sank into his skin.

*

Mandy pressed her ear to Rhys' chest, listening to the steady beat of his heart. The hard muscles of his stomach drew her fingertips and she traced their lines. She was living in a self-made hell. It wasn't an un-familiar thought. The knowledge had grown each day since the death of Rhys' father. She tried to shove from her mind the memory of the night Rhys' learned of his suicide, but it would haunt her at the oddest of times. One moment Mandy would think she would be fine, and the next, she was floored again by the night's events.

The feel of Rhys' teeth sinking into her bottom lip as he pumped inside her drove Mandy insane. Liquid heat flooded her core while tears pricked at her eyes. He'd said he loved her. She shoved the picture away. It didn't matter. In a way, it was almost as if it never happened, especially since Rhys didn't remember a second of it. In spite of her best efforts, the tears she held back slipped from her eyes and soaked Rhys' shirt beneath her cheek.

She should have known better. He'd been half out of his mind with grief and alcohol. Secretly, she suspected he'd consumed a few other things besides tequila but she couldn't prove it. When she'd intervened in his self-destruction, she should have done more to guard her heart. It was his eyes. She'd been so sure he meant every word he said to her, but then he'd woken up the next day. She cut off the thought before it decimated her again.

Mandy's stomach churned. Every day, night, and woman since then had slowly ripped away the layers of her skin. She needed to let him go. The torture of having him while not really having him needed to end. Rhys' muscles tensed beneath her, and he sucked in a deep breath.

"Are you okay, baby?"

Squeezing her eyes closed, Mandy

swallowed against the pain. His groggy voice and the fingers brushing her waist would never belong to her. "Go back to sleep." His deep breathing let her know her order had been unnecessary. Just like the night he'd taken possession of her body, he wouldn't remember this in the morning. Soon, she promised herself. She would let him go soon.

Chapter Two

Rhys' phone buzzed in the front pocket of his jeans, pulling him from his dreams. Blinking at the unfamiliar ceiling, it took him a minute to realize he was still at Mandy's. The sunlight streaming into the room and the crick in his neck spoke volumes about how long he'd slept on her couch. Glancing around, he realized Mandy was gone—most likely she'd headed for class already. The sound buzzed again and he groaned as he worked the device from his pocket. Rhys' body protested as he sat up. Making a mental note to avoid this sleeping arrangement again, he ran his finger over the screen, checking his messages. They were both from Drew. The first gave him the time of the funeral services. The second was directions to his house once he recalled Rhys had never been there before. A shot of panic raced through him until he checked the time, and his heart rate slowed. He still had enough time to run home and change before he needed to be at Drew's house.

Scrubbing at his face, Rhys shoved his phone back into his pocket as he headed for the bathroom. It wasn't until he was on his way back to the couch that he realized he'd fallen asleep before Mandy had gotten to talk to him about her business opportunity. A sinister smile tugged at his lips, and he pulled his phone out once more. It seemed he would be seeing her again today.

* * * * *

Knox sipped his coffee, wincing against the loss of his taste buds. A flash of blonde hair caught his eyes, distracting him from the pain. Mandy looked tired. It seemed in the past four weeks she'd lost weight. She didn't have the pounds to spare. Rhys wasn't taking care of her the way he should, but Knox worked hard to stay out of his brother's business. After all, it wasn't as if he was in a position to stand in judgment.

In spite of her obvious exhaustion, Mandy smiled kindly as she stepped from table to table checking on each of her customers. She helped an overwhelmed mother shuffle her children into their seats before winking at an elderly man, no doubt making the dude's day.

Knox couldn't explain why he never sat in her section or why he couldn't stay away. It had always been that way with Mandy. As if feeling his stare burning into her skin, Mandy turned and met his gaze. Just as she did every day, Mandy made her way to his table. She refilled his cup even though he didn't need it and he wasn't one of her customers.

"Knox."

"Mandy," he said, acknowledging her greeting, just as he did every day except for Sunday, since that was her day off.

Seizing his chance, Knox asked, "Why are you here instead of school?" It had been driving him nuts, but he knew it wasn't any of his concern. She froze and for the first time in memory, she focused on his face. He almost took the question back. Of all the times for him to strike up a conversation, of course he would choose the wrong topic. Story of his life.

"I had some unforeseen medical bills and I can't afford to pay my tuition any longer."

Several platitudes sprang to mind,

but each sounded as ridiculous as the last. "You were going for some sort of photography thing, right?"

"Yes but I guess we all have to come to grips with reality eventually." The acceptance of her situation didn't quite reach her eyes. Passion was a hard thing to beat into submission.

"I don't see why. I haven't."

Her mouth lifted in one corner before she turned away. As he watched her cross the room, returning to her tipping customers, he wondered if he should change sections tomorrow. He had to keep her on her toes, after all.

* * * * *

Following Drew's directions, Rhys was stunned when the red brick and tan condos came into view. He didn't know what he'd been expecting, but as a fighter who earned between two and three million dollars a year, Drew could live almost anywhere. Rhys barked out a laugh when he pulled up to the curb and spotted the two ridiculously expensive vehicles parked in the short driveway. A person needed his priorities, it seemed.

The front door opened before he had the chance to knock. Aubree smiled as she waved him inside. "I heard you pull up," she explained. Closing the door behind him, she added, "Drew is almost ready. You can blame me for making us late."

Rhys followed on her heels as she moved toward the kitchen. When she headed for the sink, he pulled a chair away from the edge of the dining room table and sat down, watching her. Her blonde curls hung down her back as she stretched above her head, reaching for a glass. After turning on the tap, she filled the cup.

"I'm in no hurry. I don't suppose the guest of honor is going anywhere." He wanted to bite his own tongue as soon as the stupid comment left his lips. Thankfully, Aubree chuckled.

"No, I don't suppose he is. I see you're a lot like your brother. You say unfortunate things when you're uncomfortable."

"Which one?" Rhys asked, attempting to hide his disbelief. He hadn't realized Aubree knew either of his siblings.

Aubree took a quick drink of water before setting her glass in the sink. She leaned her hip into the counter, turning her attention his way.

"Knox," she answered, before adding, "I didn't realize you had more than one."

Rhys worked to keep his face blank.

He should've known Knox would never speak of Dane, but hearing it confirmed left him feeling deflated. "There's a brother between Knox and me."

Aubree seemed thoughtful, making him worry he'd not done a good job of hiding his emotions, and he quickly steered the conversation in a different direction. "How do you know Knox?" As the question left his mouth, a movement over Aubree's shoulder caught Rhys's attention. He spotted Drew coming up behind Aubree through the kitchen's side door. Drew's eyes danced with humor as he motioned for Rhys to stay quiet. Rhys locked his gaze on Aubree's face, doing his best to keep from giving Drew away. With her lips pressed together and her mouth twitching, it was obvious to Rhys she knew exactly what was going on behind her. At the last second, and when it seemed Drew would finally get the drop on her, Aubree drove her elbow into Drew's gut, catching him unawares. Drew threw his head back, roaring with laughter. Aubree's blue eyes lit up with happiness, striking Rhys with a sudden insight. Drew was a lucky bastard.

Rhys had always been a people watcher. He loved observing his surroundings and gathering up all the pieces of everything around him before fitting them together until he felt as if he knew their life story as well as he did his own. Everything he'd gathered on Drew came together the moment the man touched Aubree. This tiny woman had swept the huge fighter off his feet. He'd been helpless against her. Not because of something tangible anyone would be able to see, but Rhys saw it now. Aubree possessed a soft inner beauty, directly offsetting Drew's darkness and making him better.

The small apartment kept her close at all times, while the expensive cars gave Drew an outlet to release his urge to spoil her. Not only was the pair a perfect match, they would also make amazing parents. There was too much love in their home for it to be otherwise.

Resting his chin on top of Aubree's head, Drew focused on Rhys as he absently caressed her stomach. "I thought we would take the Range Rover so we won't get separated on the drive. Since my father's body was cremated, they're having the ceremony at his home. Well, I guess it's Max's home now."

"Are you sure you're up for this?" Rhys was waiting for Drew to answer Aubree's question, but as the pair continued staring his way, he realized her inquiry had been intended for him. "I mean, you don't have to do this if you feel like it's too soon after your father's death," Aubree added, sounding worried. "I'm so bad at these things."

At her obvious discomfort, Rhys rushed to reassure her. "My father was cremated as well. It's odd, but for some reason that detail made it feel less real. It was Mandy's suggestion, and I'm still grateful for it. Don't worry over me."

* * * * *

Just as Rhys suspected, the services passed with a lingering sense of unreality. To his mind, it was hard to imagine a person inside a vase. Drew had been right to think he'd be pulled away from Aubree. It seemed everyone wanted to shake his hand or discuss something with him privately. The son his father did claim stood off to the side wearing an expression dark enough that no one dared speak to him.

Drew pointed out the man along with his friend Ryan as soon as they cleared the door, and Rhys had kept a close eye on their whereabouts at all times. He could sense Aubree doing the same thing as they sat side by side waiting for Drew to finish up.

The two men embraced, and Aubree tilted her head, appearing thoughtful as she watched them. Max was intense. There was no other way to describe his harsh expression, but he was also dry-eyed. However, his friend Ryan must have seen something in the silence no one else could because he was quick to offer comfort. Max's face softened the moment Ryan touched him, and Rhys knew. They loved each other and not in a platonic way. Rhys switched his gaze to Aubree, wondering if she'd come to the same conclusion. He was watching her face so closely he missed

Max and Ryan heading in their direction. When Aubree tilted her head back and Max spoke, Rhys silently groaned. Drew would kill them all.

"Thank you for coming."

Aubree didn't look scared. "Of course. Did you really think I wouldn't?"

Ryan and Max both stooped down so Aubree wouldn't have to keep staring up at them hovering over her. Max rubbed his hands over his thighs in a nervous gesture. "I owe you a huge apology." He cut his eyes in Rhys' direction. "Is there any way I could speak to you privately?"

"I would say yes, but Rhys will be the one who feels Drew's wrath if I send away my private security." At Aubree's answer Rhys glanced at her in shock, and she patted his knee. "Don't worry, sweetie. For all Drew's silence, he's a motor mouth at home. He couldn't keep a secret from me if his life depended upon it. Not to mention, he's too nice and his conscience gets the best of him."

Ryan cleared his throat bringing their attention back to them. "We both owe you an apology," Ryan added.

Aubree looked back and forth between the men. Rhys thought for a moment she blinked back tears, but it passed too quickly for him to be sure. "The two of you are perfect for each other. I don't know why I never noticed it before today. We see what we want, I suppose."

A sad smile touched Max's face. "It doesn't excuse what we did to you." The conversation had taken a strange turn, and Rhys no longer understood what was going on. He'd assumed Max was apologizing for hurting her, but now it seemed Ryan was sorry as well, and Rhys felt lost.

"I'm oddly relieved," Aubree admitted. "For a long time, I wondered how could you pretend to be my friends? I mean, we really were friends, and I felt as if it meant nothing to either of you. Now I understand. Love is an addiction you'll do anything to feed. Better I lost the two of you to your love than anything I imagined." She brushed her hand over her rounded stomach and smiled. "I'm sorry for your loss, and I hope you have a long, happy future together."

Max and Ryan both leaned forward, gathering Aubree into a group hug. Unfortunately, it was the exact moment Rhys caught sight of Drew heading their way, and it was obvious by the muscle twitching in his jaw he'd not missed a thing. It was almost comical the way everyone turned in Drew's direction, or it would have been funny if Rhys wasn't the one who was responsible for Aubree.

Flashing him an accusing look, Drew barked, "Get lost."

"Nope," Rhys said, adding a bright smile he did not feel. "I promised you I wouldn't let you do this."

They stared each other down and Rhys questioned his sanity. Aubree sighed, dragging everyone's attention her way. "Well, while the four of you work this out, I'm going to steal a moment to myself." Without waiting for permission, she stood and swept from the room. Drew's mouth twitched. An inner sigh of relief ran through Rhys at the sight. The small twist of his lips made Rhys realize Drew was not as angry as he let on. Drew's voice softened when he spoke again, confirming Rhys' thoughts. "It's all right, Rhys. We need to talk some shit over and I'd prefer there to be no witnesses to some of the things I need to say. You know, in case you're ever called to testify against me."

With a sharp nod, Rhys gave in. "I need to send Mandy a text anyhow, but I'll be around if you need me."

Following in Aubree's wake, Rhys headed out the door and down the long hall, but she'd already disappeared inside of one of the many rooms. The gleaming wood and lack of family pictures on the walls left the house feeling cold. In an attempt to block out any thoughts of what it must have been like to grow up in such a house, Rhys pulled his cell phone out of his jacket pocket. He nearly growled when he saw he didn't have service. Holding the phone out in front of him, he walked the length of the hall, hoping to see a signal appear. Entering the first open doorway, which turned out to be some sort of man cave, he glanced around the room. There were a few leather chairs scattered around the floor and an expensive TV hanging on one wall. A shelf filled with different- colored bottles held every type of liquor he could think of, and a massive oak bar ran the length of one side of the room. Potted plants sat on the floor at one end of the bar, allowing for entry to the back side on only one side while a row of barstools lined the front.

Circling the room, Rhys slid in behind the oak slab when signal bar flared to life on the screen of his phone. Rhys tried several different angles and when he bent over, two bars appeared. With a triumphant laugh, he settled down on the floor and leaned against the wall. He didn't waste any time typing his text to Mandy before he lost service again.

Let me know as soon as you get home so I'll know you're safe. Okay?

Rhys smiled when his phone immediately vibrated with her response.

Almost there.

The creaking of door hinges brought Rhys' head up. Ryan followed a thunderous- looking Max into the room. He tossed a cursory glance around before quietly closing the door behind him and clicking the lock in place. Rhys knew he should announce his presence, but the intense expression Max wore held him in place. It didn't seem the time to intrude upon his grief. The plants and wooden barrier hid Rhys from view. In a small attempt to allow them some privacy, he went back to texting Mandy.

Don't text and drive, but I want to hear all about your day.

The crash of glass shattering against the wall tested Rhys' willpower and he leaned over an inch to get a better view while staying out of sight. Max ripped off his jacket and tossed it onto a nearby chair. He paced around the expensive piece of leather furniture, eyeing his shoes as he went. Ryan watched the fit of temper for a moment before interceding on Max's third pass. Rhys understood both sides. Max was angry at the unfairness of life while Ryan wanted to fix things. It was what men did. If they couldn't fix something, then they raged against it. Ryan cupped Max's face between his hands, stopping the man from looking away as he whispered what Rhys imagined were words of encouragement.

There was something oddly familiar about the scene. A sense of déjà vu overcame him as he watched the pair. In an unexpected move, Max snagged the lapels of Ryan's jacket and hauled him forward.

Ryan accepted Max's punishing kiss, absorbing the man's anger and sharing his grief the only way he could. Rhys reevaluated his position, wondering once again if he should clear his throat or something, but it seemed an even worse time than before. Ryan moaned as Max backed him against the wall. The two halves of his shirt parted as Max's mouth moved from Ryan's lips to his chest, and Ryan tilted his head back. His eyes closed and a flush of arousal covered his skin. Even in his discomfort, Rhys recognized how masterfully Ryan twisted Max's grief into passion, and as he looked on, the memory slammed into his mind with lightning clarity.

The room seemed hotter than usual as he fought to breathe. He'd been half insane since the moment he learned of his father's suicide. His older brother, Dane, had given him some sort of anti-anxiety medicine right before Rhys had made the terrible decision to consume an epic amount of alcohol. The combination left him out of his head but had done nothing to cool his rage. How could his dad leave them? Even though he could hear Mandy saying his name, Rhys couldn't control the fury boiling inside him. Blood dripped from his split knuckles, and the wall of his living room would never be the same again, but he'd calmed down enough for Mandy to touch him.

She held his face between her hands, forcing him to focus on her, but Rhys couldn't understand a word she said. Even if the words wouldn't penetrate his mind, the concerned tears in her blue eyes held him in check while the touch of skin on skin caused something primal to rise inside him. He had wanted her for too long. Control was not an option.

"I love you." The look of shock on Mandy's face did nothing to deter him. "I've always loved you," he added as he buried his fingers in the hair at the nape of her neck and hauled her closer. "I need you, Mandy. Damn, I really don't think I can stand another minute without you."

Even before the final word left his lips, he was crushing her against him. Rhys spun until she was pinned between him and the wall.

Rhys' heart raced and he barely resisted the urge to drop his head between his knees to stave off a rapidly approaching panic attack. The muscles in his stomach clenched as the entire night came rushing back. He'd not been gentle with her. The phone between his fingers vibrated. Drawing his knees up, Rhys draped his arm across them and dropped his forehead on it. Staring down at the face of his phone, he read the text on the screen without absorbing a word of it.

She tasted like something sweet he couldn't identify as it mixed with the taste of the tequila he'd consumed. Her fingers fumbled with the button on his jeans as he shoved her shirt up. When she set his erection free, he lost the last ounce of sanity he had.

Tearing his mind away from the past, Rhys leaned his head against the wall. Feeling numb, he looked on as Max went down onto his knees and Ryan dropped his chin to his chest to watch. A tattoo covered Ryan's torso, and Rhys couldn't make out what it was, but he absently noted it continued down his body and over his hipbone. The man was built like a fighter, but Rhys didn't think he'd ever seen him before today. He was doing his best to concentrate on anything except his own thoughts, or what the pair of men across the room were doing. Funnily enough, he knew he could look anywhere else, but he couldn't rip his eyes away. It was the expression Ryan wore as he stared down at Max pleasuring his body. It was more than sexual.

She smelled like strawberries. It was the only thought penetrating his lust. Her moans filled his ears. Her eyes were unfocused, but she didn't look away as her orgasm hit and she squeezed his cock with her inner muscles. A drop of blood appeared on her shell-pink bottom lip from where he'd bitten it.

"I love you." The words rang out from across the room clearly enough to yank Rhys from the memory of Mandy's heat. He could barely see Ryan now with Max boxing him in with his arms braced on either side of him on the wall, but Rhys recognized it had been his voice. Max touched his lips to Ryan's briefly before a sound somewhere between a growl and sigh escaped him.

"I really want all these goddamn people to leave."

"Do you want me to tell them to go away? I'm not above making a serious ass of myself if it will make you happy."

Max released a low chuckle. "You make me happy. You are the only fucking thing in this world that matters to me."

There was a tension-filled moment

of silence where even the room seemed to hold its breath as the pair stared each other down. Ryan was the first to break. "Just not in front of Drew, I take it?"

Max pushed away from the wall with a frustrated snarl. Rhys caught a flash of hurt crossing over Ryan's face before he dropped his gaze, carefully concentrating on buttoning his pants and shirt. Max scrubbed his hands over his head.

"I froze, okay? When he demanded my side of the story, I didn't know what to say. He caught me off guard, but I'm not ashamed."

"Yep. Gotcha," Ryan said, sounding devoid of all emotion.

"Goddamn it, Ryan," Max roared, crowding him against the wall again. "I swear I am not ashamed. I don't know how to be his brother and I sure as hell don't know how to talk to him about how I feel," he admitted as he leaned closer. "I love you so damn much," he added as he opened his mouth over Ryan's. Rhys' chest tightened at the words.

The blaring light streaming through his bedroom window felt like an axe landing in the center of his forehead. Luckily, the smell of the coffee wafting from the cup Mandy set on the bedside table didn't cause his stomach to churn. There were smudges underneath her eyes. She smiled when she noticed he was awake. "It lives," she said quietly as if she realized how much his head hurt. She leaned over him, smiling, and his eyes locked on the cut on her bottom lip. Reaching up, he brushed his fingers over it and caught sight of the dried blood on his knuckles. He felt sick after all.

"What happened to your lip? Please tell me I didn't hit you?"

An odd look crossed over her face, and her voice came out sounding strained. "No. You beat up your living room wall. The lip is my fault."

Relief washed through him. "Thank God. How did I get home from the bar? I don't remember a thing after the first hour."

Mandy turned her face away and fidgeted with the cup of coffee. "Dane called me and I picked you up." Eyeing her white t-shirt and pajama pants, he guessed she'd been in a hurry to get him before he did something stupid.

"Did you show up in this?" he asked as he toyed with the hem of her shirt.

Watching her profile, he saw her swallow hard before answering. "Yeah." She gazed around the room. "If you're going to be okay, I need to go home and change. I'll be quick so I can take you to the funeral home today in order for you and your both-ers to, you know..." She waved her hand. He didn't want her to leave, but the knowledge she would be with him while he helped make his father's final arrange-ments soothed him. She brushed her hair over her shoulder and he could swear she blinked back tears.

"Are you okay?"

Mandy nodded. "I'm just worried about you." She punctuated her answer with a fake smile, and he knew it was for his benefit. He vowed he'd be stronger for her.

He was such an ass. She must have been devastated. The walls began closing in on him, but he noticed the door now stood open and the men were gone. He started to push himself from the floor when Aubree's head appeared over the edge, causing his heart to jump into this throat. "There you are. I saw Max and Ryan leave." A luminous smile stretched across her face. "Were you treated to a show?"

Rhys winced at the question. "Unfortunately, yes."

She snorted with laughter at his answer. "I've been in the middle of one of those episodes. It was pretty hot from what I recall."

Rhys concentrated on brushing the dust from his clothes as he stood to hide his surprise. Aubree's confession cleared away a thousand questions in his mind but added a few more. He decided on an innocent one. "How did you know I was back here?"

Aubree settled onto one of the barstools and waved her hand dismissively. "I saw you come in here, and I started to join you before Max stormed in. Once Ryan closed the door, I figured I'd better wait. When they left, I put two and two together. This place is like some sort of black hole of cell service, and—believe it or not—I've hovered back there to make a call before myself. Did you get Mandy?"

Her question reminded him of the waiting message he'd not really seen earlier. He glanced at the screen again before answering. "Yeah. She just got home from work."

Resting her chin on her hand, Aubree watched him for so long he barely stopped himself from fidgeting. When her question came, it was almost a relief. "You are sick with wanting her, aren't you?"

Although Rhys had known in the back of his mind it would take an amazing woman to have captured Drew the way Aubree had, he was still in awe. He could tell she wasn't judging or digging for information. She understood. After a moment, he nodded. "She's the one."

"Then it's time for you to shit or get off the pot."

A bark of laughter escaped Rhys. "My grandmother would have loved you. She used to say the same thing all the time."

"She sounds like she was a smart lady. Seriously, though, you need to move in on Mandy before she gets away. Surely you don't think no one else is interested?"

"I have a plan," he said, telling himself it wasn't a complete lie. He did intend to force her hand this weekend, especially now.

"Is it of the five-year variety?"

He shook his head in disbelief at her snarky comeback.

Drew appeared in the doorway with

Ryan and Max in tow. "There you are. I've been looking for the two of you. I even enlisted help," he said pointing at the men behind him. Rhys shot a panicked look in Aubree's direction but she didn't as much as flinch.

"I dragged Rhys outside with me for a few minutes. There's too much testosterone flying around in the house. It's not good for the baby."

Rhys' phone vibrated, saving him from choking on her blatant lie. He stared at the screen, reading the message three times before the horror of what he was seeing set in and his temper burst out.

"Fuck! Fuck! Fuck!"

Aubree jumped at his outburst. "What?"

"Goddamn it, I have to go. I'm sorry."

"What?" Aubree repeated. "What's

happened?"

Stuffing his phone in his pocket, he pressed the heels of his hands to his eyes until he saw stars. Dropping his hands, he met Drew's gaze across the room. "Dane is at Mandy's house tearing the place apart." He could hear the bleak note in his voice. He sounded tired even to him.

"I'll go with you," Drew offered without hesitation. "What about Aubree? You don't want her there."

Drew switched his gaze between him and Aubree. Rhys could see how torn he was. He wanted to help but he equally didn't want to leave Aubree with Max. Rhys rushed to settle the matter. "Don't worry about it. I've dealt with Dane alone many times."

"You shouldn't have to," Aubree argued.

Max cut into the conversation.

66

"We'll take Aubree home."

There was a moment when Rhys thought Drew might pop a blood vessel, before he snarled. "Like hell."

"They won't hurt me, but if you're worried over it, I'll just go with you two." Aubree was trying to be helpful, but her timing was awful, as far as Rhys was concerned. Max looked away as if her words physically hurt him. She was absolving him of guilt, but it didn't seem as if he felt he deserved it. Drew was eyeing the room like a caged animal, and Rhys didn't have time for their shit.

"Oh for the love of," Rhys growled, cutting off his own curse. The picture of Dane terrorizing Mandy rose in his mind and something inside him snapped. Slamming his fist down on the wooden surface, he caused everyone to jump, but he had their attention. "This is fucking ridiculous.

I don't know the whole story and I don't care. What I do know is I have to go, and your stupid bullshit is standing in my way. Aubree, you cannot go to this, my brother is crazy. Drew, I'm fine to go alone. I can call for a ride, but if you're going, then your wife will be fine with Max. Max, quit being a pussy. Drew couldn't care fucking less if you're in love with Ryan, and as a matter of fact, the knowledge would go a long way to smoothing things over. If Drew understands anything, it's how insane being in love with someone makes a person. Does everybody have it? Can I fucking go now?"

Halfway through his speech, Aubree covered her mouth as if she couldn't believe what she was hearing and Max had frozen up like a block of ice. A look of confusion passed over Drew's features before everything seemed to fall into place inside his mind, and he merely looked stunned. Ryan was the only person in the room who appeared unaffected by it all. Rhys realized he was probably one hell of a poker player.

Drew gave a decisive nod. "All right, let's go." He leaned over and pressed a quick kiss to Aubree's lips before shooting a hard look at Max. "I'm trusting you here. Don't make me sorry." Without waiting for a response, he headed for the door, waving for Rhys to follow.

* * * * *

Knox kept one eye locked on the road as he dug around in the console searching for the ringing cell phone. He hated technology. When he finally managed to snag it, he flipped on the hands-free speaker.

"Hello?"

"Hey man, it's Max. I hate calling you with this shit, but Dane is over at

Mandy's tearing her place apart." Black spots floated across Knox's vision. "Are you still there?"

"Yeah," Knox said, gripping the wheel until he thought something would snap. "Do you have an address for me?"

"Um, hold on." He could hear a muffled conversation going on in the background before Max's voice came through clear again. "Aubree has it. Are you ready?"

"Yep."

Max rattled off an address, and Knox drove across the median when he realized he was going the wrong way. "Thanks for letting me know. I'll take care of it."

The calm note to his voice belied the rage seething under his skin. Knox had given up on Dane years ago, but this was too fucking much. Traffic moved at a snail's pace, adding fuel to his anger. Several times, he considered running a few cars off the road when they didn't move out his way quickly enough. By the time her apartment building came into view, he was grinding his back teeth to pulp and he could hear the blood rushing in his ears.

The two parking spaces in front of her door were already occupied. He recognized Mandy's car as one and the other was a black Range Rover, which appeared to be brand new. The doors of the SUV and the door to Mandy's apartment stood open. Before Knox could find a place to park, Drew appeared in the doorway with his arms around Dane as he hauled him outside.

Pulling into the first empty spot, Knox watched the show, torn between helping out and wondering why Drew was there. He didn't see Dane's car, and he assumed the expensive Range Rover belonged to Drew. After a few minutes of Drew going nose-to-nose with Dane, his brother went limp. Damn, he hated this shit. He'd spent so many years physically subduing their father every time he went into an alcohol- or drug-induced rage. If Drew had this, then more power to him. Knox would not waste another day on it. The sun glimmered off Mandy's hair as she appeared in the doorway, dragging his gaze her way. Knox's mouth fell open in surprise when her fist landed in the center of Dane's face.

Relaxing in his seat, Knox felt a smile tug at the corners of his mouth. It didn't seem he was needed after all, but he'd wait to make sure she was safe all the same.

* * * * *

If Drew was the least bit concerned over breaking every traffic law known to man, Rhys couldn't tell. He'd shut down his emotions again, and Rhys couldn't get a read on him any longer. On the other side of the spectrum, when they arrived at Mandy's apartment it was to find Dane as crazed as only a person with a ton of drugs in his system could be. Mandy's door stood open and her screams could be heard even with the doors of the SUV still closed. Dane sprang away from Mandy wild-eyed as Rhys cleared the entryway. His short blond hair stood on end and sweat coated his skin.

"You said you'd be here," Dane accused. His gaze bounced from wall to wall as if he searched for an escape. "She said you weren't. I thought she was lying. I just wanted her to stop lying." Dane's voice rose with each word.

Mandy appeared unnaturally calm. Rhys' heart twisted at her expression. She was gone. He knew the countenance all too well. He saw it each time he looked at Knox. It was total mental blockage of the world.

Keeping a level voice, he did his best to soothe Dane. "I'm here now."

"But you weren't fucking here when I needed you!"

Mandy flinched and Drew struck, easily plucking Dane from his spot on the floor while somehow managing to keep him subdued as he carried him outside.

On wooden legs, Mandy walked into the kitchen and came back carrying the broom. No matter how hard Rhys tried, she refused to look at him, and he bit back the urge to force her. The red splotches on her arms told him too much. He didn't want to know, but he needed to.

"Talk to me, please?" She swiped at the mess. "Damn it, Mandy. What the hell happened here?"

She went from zoned out to an explosion of fury in an instant. Flinging the broom away from her, she turned on him. "I'm tired, Rhys. I'm so fucking sick of cleaning up after you. You parade women into my work, and your brother—" She bit off her words as if the rage was becoming too much. With a helpless shrug, she tried again. "I'm fed up with always being there for you while I'm obviously easily forgotten." As if saying the words hardened something inside her, Mandy stood straighter and she brushed past him. Even as his heart twisted in his chest, Rhys tried to reach for her but she swatted his hands away. He wanted to fix it. The thought of Dane harming her in any way left him half-crazed. His skin itched, feeling almost too tight for his body, making him want to crawl out of it.

Nausea ate at his gut as he followed her to the door. She'd never been angry with him before, and he was at a loss as to how to make things right. Dane appeared in the open doorway, but Mandy's step did not falter. He focused on her with shame etched in his every feature. Drew hovered over his shoulder, poising to strike if Dane flipped out again, but Rhys knew from experience the outbursts were usually short-lived.

Dane stammered an apology, but in a flash and taking everyone by surprise, Mandy landed a solid blow to the center of his face. A stunned silence hung in the air as Mandy shook out her knuckles. Dane bent at the waist, clutching his face with both hands, hissing in pain. The crazed look in Mandy's eye scared the hell out of Rhys. He'd never seen her like this.

"If you ever come near me again, I will cut off your balls. Do you understand me?" The spite in her voice added truth to her promise. Holding each of their gazes long enough to prove how serious she was, Mandy added, "I want you gone. All of you need to leave."

Dane tried to speak through his fingers, but his excuses fell on deaf ears as Mandy snarled, "Now!"

Drew shoved Dane toward the SUV, pausing only long enough for the man to spit blood on the sidewalk. When Rhys was sure Drew had things under control, he moved toward Mandy, but she pointed at the vehicle.

"I'm not playing. You need to fucking leave."

Desperation boiled in his skin. He

could not lose the only good thing he had. "Please talk to me?"

Mandy threw her arms wide and turned in a circle. "Look at my apartment, Rhys. Look at me," she added, pointing out the bruises rapidly rising on her arms. "Do you know how much I struggle for everything I have? Between going to school all day and working all night, I have nothing." She let out a mirthless laugh. "All I've ever done is love you, and all you do is wreck me."

He clenched his back teeth against the pain on her face and the hurt slashing across his heart. When his jaw cracked under the strain, he forced it to relax. She deserved the truth. "You've always owned my heart. I can't lose you. I love you too much."

She met his stare and Rhys saw something in her eyes he never expected.

It looked a lot like hate. "You only love me when it's convenient to do so, and I don't want it."

*

Mandy wrapped her anger around her heart as she swept the glass into the dustpan. In truth, she'd been more scared than pissed off when Dane burst through her door, but once she began the argument with Rhys, she couldn't stop. All the hurt and growing bitterness she'd nursed since his father's death erupted at one time. It was almost as if a dam opened up inside her. As much as she'd known her heart was silently breaking, she'd not realized how much it was poisoning her soul until she was tossing Rhys' love back in his face.

Her thoughts were firmly locked on their confrontation and adrenaline still raced through her veins, making her heart jumped into her throat when the solid knock landed on her front door. Her hands shook as she threw it open, prepared to go another round with Rhys, only to find Knox standing there instead. At six foot five, Knox was the largest of the Collier brothers. His shaggy brown hair, green eyes, hard body, and tattoos caused women to stop and stare everywhere he went. The dark scowl and menacing vibe rolling off him kept any of those women from doing anything other than fantasizing.

Mandy's surprise over his appearance had her stepping back, allowing him entrance before she realized what she'd done. Deciding it was too late to back down, she chose instead to brazen it out.

"As you can see, your brothers have been here," she said, waving toward the mess surrounding her.

Knox nodded. "I heard. Drew's brother called me."

The statement wiped away her anxiety over his presence, replacing it with curiosity and giving her something to focus on. "You know Drew's brother?"

He shrugged at her question. "I know a lot of people I shouldn't."

Mandy wasn't surprised. Knox was the type of person who kept his mouth shut, his ears open, and his business to himself. As long as she'd known him, she still wasn't sure what he did for a living. He entered the occasional fight but not enough to support himself financially. She went back to cleaning, expecting he would say his bit while she worked. Instead, he silently began helping her.

"I suppose I'll get a different call any day now," he said absently as he picked up several pictures from the floor and hung them back on the wall. "Each time I answer the phone, I brace myself for the news of Dane's death. It was the same with my dad. I must've had a thousand conversations with strangers, police and hospital staff before I got the final call informing me there was nothing they could do to save him."

Without realizing it, Mandy stopped working and sat down, giving Knox her full attention. "I've cleaned up a hundred messes exactly like this one," he added as he shook the glass out of one of the frames into a trash bag. "I'll get you a new one of these," he said as he hung the frame back on the wall.

"Don't worry over it. I got it at the dollar store."

Setting the bag aside, Knox picked up the broom she'd abandoned and swept away the remnants of damage. Mandy automatically lifted her feet and set them on the edge of the coffee table as he swiped at the hardwood in front of her chair. She knew she should feel guilty over watching as he cleaned her house, but she was fascinated. As far as Mandy knew, Knox had never spoken openly about his life.

"I guess it will only cost me a dollar to replace it, then," he said after a few minutes, making Mandy wonder if he'd become so lost in his own thoughts, he was just now catching up in their conversation.

"I have a stack of them in the closet." She wasn't sure why she continued to argue over something as trivial as a dollar picture frame, but she did.

Knox avoided her gaze. "All you have to do is say 'don't buy me anything', and I won't."

Even though his tone never changed, Mandy got the impression he was angry with her for not being straight-forward. "Fine," she said, giving in. "Don't buy me anything."

She could tell he was smiling by the way his profile shifted, but he still wouldn't look at her. "You know, I'm not surprised you and Rhys can't get your shit together," he said, surprising her with the change in topic. "Both of you are so damn stubborn."

"I have no idea what you're talking about."

He ignored her lie. "You want him to be simple and speak up about his feelings. He wants to be that person too, but he's not. Proving he's a true product of our up-bringing, Rhys isn't sure which move he should make. He only knows it will be the wrong one."

With nothing left to sweep, Knox sat down on the couch. When he finally looked directly at her, Mandy fought the urge to glance away. In spite of his present openness, his eyes were hard. Although she didn't believe it was any reflection of his feelings toward her, Mandy was unaccustomed to dealing with someone as emotionally disconnected as Knox.

Fortunately, he didn't wait for her to deny it. "Our grandmother used to tell us, every single day, people only want what they can't have, and they're never happy with what they've got. I thought at the time she was trying to get us ready to deal with real life. Turns out she was preparing us to handle the reality of our father because we were what he had." Knox scoffed at his own words. "People think Rhys turned out to be the least damaged out of our household, but I know the truth. He's every bit as fucked up as the rest of us. How could he not be?" Without waiting for her to answer, he added, "If you've never been good enough to hang on to anyone, including your own parents, it does something to your mind. Then he meets you. The desperation to keep you in any capacity must be almost crippling."

Mandy dropped her gaze to her lap. Her chest hurt as she rubbed absently at the bruises on her arms. In the end, she knew there was no way she would be able to avoid the truth forever, but she never expected how much it would break her heart to say the words aloud. "Six weeks ago, I had a miscarriage, and last night I served dinner to Rhys' date. Today, I dished out her lunch while she regaled me with the story of how Rhys rocked her world before coming over to sleep on my couch."

As the confession left her lips, she couldn't stop the bitterness and pain from leaking out as well. In an attempt to harden her heart against it, she locked her teeth together and lifted her chin. She caught a flash of shock passing over Knox's face before his usual mask fell back in place. It was Mandy's undoing because along with his surprise, she'd also caught a glimpse of what Knox kept hidden behind his hardened veneer. She swallowed against the tears trying to escape.

Knox cleared his throat twice, as if searching for the right words. Finally, he said, "I'm assuming my brother doesn't know."

Mandy snorted. "He doesn't even remember." She lifted her hands helplessly before dropping them back in her lap. "I'm just…I'm so fucking angry, Knox. I have all this inside me, and I don't..." she began, but without warning, the will to fight left her, and she lost the battle against her emotions. Her teeth chattered and she couldn't stop shaking.

Every wall around Knox fell. He was unrecognizable as he moved to sweep her from her chair. When they were completely unguarded, the resemblance between the brothers was shocking. It only made her cry harder as he wrapped her in his arms.

Mandy cried until there were no more tears and then she cried some more. When she was completely exhausted, she was surprised to find her head in Knox's lap. He ran his fingers through her hair, as if comforting a child. She knew she should move away, but she couldn't.

"Why do you hide?"

She didn't expound on her question,

and Knox didn't pretend to misunderstand. "You don't want to know me, and you shouldn't trust me."

"Why?" His fingers froze in her hair at the question, and she didn't think he'd answer. She was amazed when he did.

"I don't even want to know me, and I sure as hell don't trust myself."

"I'll trust you until you give me a reason not to," she told him, causing him to release a low chuckle.

"You won't have long to wait."

* * * * *

Eyes are the window to the soul. It was an overly used sentiment, but Knox and his brothers had been force-fed adages by their grandmother every day until she died. Eye contact was intimate. A meeting of two spirits. It was something he didn't do unless he was squaring off against someone. With Mandy, he never wanted to look away. He took great care to avoid most people, except her. Her gaze was addictive and it belonged to his brother. It was a fact he reminded himself of daily.

Each time he caught sight of the bruises forming on her arms, a murderous rage rolled through him. No one touched her, not even his brother. Dragging a deep breath through his nose, he counted slowly to ten. She trusted him. Why? He turned the question over in his mind in hopes of cooling his temper. Rhys would never forgive him if he killed Dane. Damn, he really wanted to kill Dane.

Silky locks continued slipping through his fingers. Her breathing deepened. His stomach tightened. The idea of her being alone, angry, hurting or struggling in any way seemed wrong on so many levels. Light flowed from her and brightened the lives of the people around her. She deserved better. What the fuck was wrong with Rhys? In spite of all the things he'd said to her, Knox couldn't understand why his brother would fail her in every aspect the way he had. He had the world right there at his fingertips. Only a fool would ignore such a possibility.

Rolling over, Mandy made a snuffling sound in her sleep. She snuggled closer and he tried hard to ignore the way her hand fell across his midsection. Rhys was more than a fool. He was a freaking idiot. Unable to stop himself from doing so, Knox ran his finger down the line of her cheek.

He would do what he could. Maybe he couldn't take away the pain of her loss or force Rhys to grow a brain, but he would do whatever it took. As long as she was happy, nothing else mattered. He waited until he could no longer feel his legs and he was sure she wouldn't wake up before slipping out from beneath her. After a quick search, Knox found a thick blanket to cover her. Another exploration of the room turned up a pen and a spiral notebook. Scratching out a quick note, he left his cell number with her in case she needed anything else before letting himself out.

Knox held out until he was behind the wheel of his truck before digging out his phone and pulling up the number he needed. After two rings, a chipper female answered his call. "Thanks for calling Grid Iron. How may I help you?"

"Hey Kerry. It's Knox."

"Hey darling. What can I do for you?"

"Are you still friends with the woman who works in the billing department at the hospital? The one who helped you ruin some girl's credit back when she cheated on your brother?" he clarified, in case she knew more than one girl who worked there. "Hell yeah! Those are the kind of go-to-jail-with-you friends you keep for life."

Even though she couldn't see him, Knox still nodded his approval. "Good. I'm calling in a favor."

Chapter Three

Knox dumped his gym bag on the floor and twisted the lid off his bottle of water as he claimed the treadmill beside Rhys. As the oldest of the three brothers, Knox had been the first to shut down when their home life fell apart. Rhys didn't believe for a moment his brother had intentionally closed them out, but the damage had been the same. With their mother gone and their father drowning his sorrows, Rhys and Dane were left without a place to turn. An older sibling was better than nothing, but Knox became a stranger and they all drifted apart.

"Wow. Miracles never cease. What brings you in today?"

"Sparring with Drew," Knox answered without looking at him. "Did you get Dane straightened out?"

Rhys didn't bother asking how Knox had heard about Dane. Knox always knew everything. "Yeah. He agreed to give rehab another shot, so I got him settled in last night. Luckily, no real harm was done." Knox grunted but didn't say anything in response. As much as Rhys should have been accustomed to his brother's silence, he wasn't.

After two deep pulls on his water and several uncomfortable glances his way, Rhys was ready to crawl out of his skin. "Damn, say what you have to say already," he growled without breaking stride.

Turning the bottle up, Knox finished off the contents. He spent a moment staring off into space and tapping the empty bottle against his thigh. Since Knox was wearing jeans, he assumed his brother didn't have any intention of using the machine he was on, but he also didn't seem to be moving toward any type of conversation either. Rhys was trying to decide if he was gathering his thoughts or intentionally annoying him when Knox finally spoke. "You're a fucking idiot."

"Never mind, I've decided I don't want to hear what you have to say after all," Rhys said dryly, and Knox let out a snort of laughter. His green eyes shone with mirth, but the wry smile twisting his lips told a different story.

"If only I was joking. Unfortunately, I'm very serious. Out of the three of us, you're the biggest ass, and that is saying something."

"Awesome. Thanks for the love. See you next year around this time."

Knox shook his head at Rhys' sarcastic tone, but he didn't leave. "Can I ask you a question? You have to be brutally honest in your answer, not for me, but for yourself."

Giving in, Rhys shut down his machine and gave Knox his complete attention. "Sure. Why not?"

"Let me start by saying I know you care about Mandy, and for real, she cares about you too. The world would be blown away if the two of you didn't end up together, but lately I have been wondering about something. Are you her friend or is she yours?"

"What kind of shit question is that? We are friends, or were, if Dane didn't totally fuck it up for life," Rhys added bitterly.

Knox nodded slowly. "Then I suppose you know she's dropped out of college to take up more hours at Black River?" Rhys could only stare at Knox in disbelief.

Knox glanced away. "Yeah, I thought as much."

"There's no way. She would have said something," he said as soon as his voice returned. "She did say she had a business opportunity for me, but everything blew up before I had a chance to find out what it was."

Jumping off the treadmill, Knox threw his water bottle into a nearby trashcan before returning to Rhys' side. "Look, I know you feel as if I abandoned you, and maybe I did." He ran his hand through his hair before starting again. "I had eight years with Mom. You were too young to remember her, but I do. For eight years, I had a loving parent, a safe home. I'm not angry she left. Dad beat her down until it was her or us. That doesn't make it right or okay, but I understand. As far as you knew, our home was normal, but I couldn't get out of there fast enough. By the time I was old enough to leave, something inside me—" He broke off, leaving Rhys wondering what he'd planned to say. Knox glanced down at his feet and cleared his throat before meeting Rhys' stare once more. "I don't know how to bridge this gap between us, and I don't have the energy for another addict. I know I suck as a brother, so think of this as tough love." Reaching behind him, he pulled a folded stack of papers from his back pocket. "I can't lecture you on the error of walking away from someone when they need you, but I can force you to open your eyes to the grief you were too self-absorbed to see. After all, this," he said as he stuffed the papers into the cup holder of Rhys' treadmill, "was your loss too."

Without another word, he scooped up his gym bag and walked away, leaving

Rhys staring after him in confusion. Knox had always been a puzzle but this was still the most bizarre encounter they'd ever had. Shaking his head, Rhys unfolded the pages he left behind. The first thing to catch his eye was Mandy's name. From there, he couldn't understand what he was looking at. It was a list of medical terms he'd never heard of before. He did know it was a bill of staggering proportions. Switching back to the first page, he read each line carefully. A terrible sense of foreboding rose inside him. By the time he reached the final detail, he could no longer breathe.

The sound of his heart beating in his ears drowned out all other noises. His vision darkened at the edges. Leaning over, he braced his elbows on the treadmill's program shelf and stared at the proof in his hands until he was sure every aspect burned into his memory. The dates matched up. His baby. The words beat at his brain until he dropped his head onto his forearms. Mandy had lost their baby, and he deserved the hatred he'd seen in her eyes.

* * * * *

No real harm was done. Seriously? What the fuck was wrong with Rhys? Anger over his brother's stupidity unfocused Knox long enough for Drew to land a lucky blow to the left side of his face. *Fuck. That hurt.* He refused to show it.

"Wake up!" Jimmy barked from the outside of the cage. "That kind of shit will get you killed." Knox mentally agreed with the elderly trainer. Shaking it off, Knox kicked out, making contact with Drew's ribs before he could block it. Drew flinched but stayed on his feet.

"Point!" The man was a tough son of

a bitch. The flash of blows coming his way was the only indication the strike had pissed Drew off. Knox managed to deflect. Barely. It was a distraction move. Knox realized it a moment too late as Drew swept his legs out from beneath him. The impact of the mat rushing up to meet him knocked the air from his lungs. Without hesitating, Drew pinned him down and rotated his arm at an odd angle behind him. He'd have to get up earlier in the morning. At the last second, Knox stopped himself from head-butting Drew across the jaw. Shit. He hated No Rival's bullshit rules. Instead of attempting to out-muscle him, Knox went limp, throwing Drew off balance. When his hold slackened, Knox twisted out from beneath him. Jimmy laughed.

"Hell yeah, Knox. Don't let him show you up. Teach him how the real men fight." Knox didn't give Drew a second chance to unbalance him. Springing forward, he leapt and landed a knee to Drew's gut. When Drew bowed slightly from the collision, Knox used the forward momentum to flip him to the mat.

"Point!" Jimmy yelled.

Drew rolled back onto his feet before Knox could pin him. A fine sheen of sweat covered Knox's body, and his muscles burned from their struggle. Drew was one of the few people who matched him in size. The bastard was heavy as hell. Balancing on the balls of his feet, Knox poised to strike, determined to take him out with a final blow.

"Time!"

"Damn it, Jimmy," Knox cursed as he spit his mouth guard onto the floor. Unfazed by his show of temper, Jimmy shrugged.

"Them's the rules, boy."

Knox grunted at being called a boy, but he let the old man slide. The ruddy-faced, white-haired ex-boxer had been Knox's trainer since the day he'd turned sixteen. He was the closest thing Knox had to a father figure, which considering Jimmy's list of bad habits, wasn't saying much.

"You're good. I imagine I'll lose my strap if you ever decide to go legal."

Knox snorted at Drew's compliment. "Legal is for pussies."

Drew roared with laughter, and Knox's eyebrows shot to his hairline. He couldn't recall ever seeing Drew smile, much less laugh. To hide his shock, he accepted the towel Jimmy offered before the man wandered off to harass a group of young pups who were lifting weights. He winced as he swiped the cloth over his eyes. Yep. Another black eye.

"How's Mandy?"

The question caught Knox unpre-pared and he froze. When the wheels in his brain started spinning again, he shrugged. "How should I know?" Knox kept his gaze averted in case his lie showed there. Prov-ing he wasn't one for swallowing down bullshit, Drew scoffed.

"Don't play dumb. I saw you sitting in the parking lot yesterday."

Damn. Busted. "She's pissed."

"Yeah. I saw as much for myself."

In spite of himself, Knox laughed quietly as he tossed the towel aside. "She has one hell of a right hook."

"I worried once the shock wore off she would realize she was hurt worse than anyone knew at the time. I didn't check on her since I knew you would. What are you going to do?"

Drew's sudden change in topic left Knox confused. "There's nothing to do. Dane is back in rehab." He shrugged. "I guess it's over."

"I mean, about Rhys."

Knox's mind went blank. "As far as I know, he doesn't need rehab."

If laughter was a surprise, Drew rolling his eyes nearly floored Knox. "Fine. It's none of my business. I will say this—I like Rhys a lot. He's a good guy, but I like Mandy too, and more importantly, Aubree adores Mandy. If my wife is unhappy, it irritates me."

"Does this have a point?"

Drew nodded solemnly, causing the overhead light to glitter across the thin layer of sweat on his bald head. "Mandy is too nice for Rhys. Misery is at the end of that road."

"Then I guess the road is at its end."

Without offering more, Knox added, "I don't remember you being this chatty."

The man wouldn't be deterred. "I'll let you in on a secret. I swiped Aubree from my brother without an ounce of guilt. Best trophy I ever earned, as a matter of fact."

"Your brother prefers men, so...I can't imagine it was real hard."

Drew threw his hands up with a growl. "Has everyone known about Max except for me?"

"I imagine so, yes." A bit proud of himself for throwing Drew off topic, Knox gathered up this things. He wanted Mandy. The desperation stayed with him at all times, but things were fucked up. If Rhys could fix shit with her, then maybe they could be happy together and Knox would resign himself to things the way he always did.

"I had a point," Drew said, reaching out to stop him from leaving. Knox pasted on his most patient expression before giving Drew his full concentration.

"Do you plan to get to it soon?" Knox tried hard to keep his exasperation from showing in his tone without success.

Dipping his chin, Drew continued. "I knew Aubree belonged with me the moment I set eyes on her. I can't explain it. For real, I'm not about to get emotional with you and shit, but I knew. I don't think it would have mattered to me who she was with. There is no low I would not have stooped to, and you're in the same position I was in. He's going to get pissed. No doubt about it. But you know what's up. You hear me?"

"Yeah, I hear you," Knox agreed. Damn. He couldn't remember ever feeling so uncomfortable.

Drew's face turned hard. "Don't let my wife have time to get upset over this. Waiting is for pussies."

A low chuckle fell from Knox's lips. "Never let it be said I made a pregnant lady unhappy."

* * * * *

Knox made it two days before showing up at her door. The black eye refused to recede, but it turned out the need to see her outweighed any thoughts of vanity. A half-smile played at the corner of Mandy's mouth when she answered the door. She belonged to his brother, Knox reminded himself harshly. Her eyes were sucking him in and making him forget again. He handed her the plastic bag dangling between his fingers. Instead of reaching for it, she took a step back, allowing him inside.

"I told you not to buy me anything."

"Yeah, about that, I don't give a fuck," he said as he set the bag filled with picture frames on her kitchen table. She inched toward the bag, peeking in.

With a laugh, she tore the plastic wrap from the top picture frame and pried the metal tabs away from the cardboard. She practically danced in place with her happiness. "I love these," she said, as if admitting a terrible secret. "I know it's ridiculous."

"It's not. Pictures are your thing." She flashed a grateful grin his way. "Have you heard from Rhys?"

"Not a word. Why?" she asked absently. *One. Two. Three.* The count slowly ticked away in his mind. When he reached fourteen, he decided Rhys had been given enough time to get his shit together. One man's loss...

"He said you had a business opportunity for him."

Mandy's hands froze. "I did," she answered slowly. "I was approached by a sports magazine about a photography position they have opening up. Unfortunately, they want to see a portfolio, which I have, but they want sports models. I don't have that. I'd planned to offer him the thousand dollars I have left in my savings if he'd let me build a collection of photographs around him." She shrugged as if it didn't matter, but he knew it did.

"He's not your only connection."

She pulled a face. "I could ask Drew, but I don't feel comfortable doing so. Not to mention, a thousand dollars is probably a laughable amount to him. Rhys has the body and wouldn't scoff at the money. I guess I thought even if he had a few qualms, he'd be willing to do it for me. You know, because he cared." She returned to popping the back off the frame, and the pain of realizing Rhys did not care showed even in her posture.

"I could do it." The offer left his lips before he knew he would make it. She winced and he wished he could take it back.

"I have zero desire to go to No Rival," she explained, soothing away his ire. It made sense she wouldn't want to risk running into Rhys.

"We wouldn't need to. I only keep my membership with them so I can watch the fight list. You know, in case I see one I'd like to get in on, and sometimes I spar with Drew for the fun of it. But I don't usually workout or train there."

"Really?"

The hopeful note in her voice settled the matter. He was doing this. "Yeah. I go

to Grid Iron. It's closer to my house."
Warming up to the idea, he added, "Max
and Ryan teach a few classes there. I'm
sure they wouldn't mind if you snuck in
some shots of them as well. It would add
to the diversity of your portfolio."

He wasn't above using her dream
against her to get his way. Mandy's face
brightened for a moment before falling
again.

"I can't afford to pay three people."

"I don't want your money and Max's
dad left him everything. I don't think it will
be an issue." If it did turn out to be an issue, then he would pay them. Of course,
he didn't say as much to her. Mandy
chewed on her bottom lip. He could feel
her caving. "How many other candidates
will have three models at their disposal?"
He knew he was throwing everything he
had at her, but he was determined to win.

113

A smile stretched across Mandy's face and a mischievous glint lit her eyes. He was captivated. "You'd have to be willing to show some skin."

Without thought, Knox pulled his shirt over his head, baring his torso. A blush touched her cheeks. He dared her with his eyes to show him any weakness. Satisfaction roared through him when she took up his challenge, dropping her gaze to his chest. His nostrils flared as a sudden realization punched him in the gut. He wouldn't stop until he had her. Writhing, moaning, and pinned beneath him. The knowledge stunned him to the point he didn't move away when her cool fingers touched his ribs. Electricity surged through him where their skin met. He'd never truly believed he had a chance with her before that moment.

"Holy crap. Should I even bother

asking what you've been doing?"

He didn't waste any energy by looking down at the black bruise covering one side of his body as he answered. "No." He cursed himself as an idiot for not thinking before removing his shirt.

"Does it hurt?"

Her concern caused his throat to burn, and his voice came out sounding low. "Do I pass the test?" Lifting her chin, their gazes collided. Standing this close, he noticed her blue eyes had a touch of brown streaking through them.

"When can we get started?"

Such an open-ended question from such an innocent woman had Knox stepping away. He shoved his arms inside his shirt and pulled it back over his head while avoiding her stare.

"Since Sundays are your day off, I'll pick you up then."

She didn't ask how he knew her schedule, and without thinking, he touched his lips to her cheek. The sound of her breath catching at the back of her throat only added fuel to the fire. Heading for the door without a backward glance, he prayed she didn't attempt to stop him. He could not be trusted to stay.

* * * * *

The lighting at Grid Iron was perfect for a photo shoot. The freshly painted white walls shimmered under the bright fluorescent lights. Thick padding covered the floor of the private room where kickboxing classes were held nightly. Max and Ryan were both gorgeous and offset one another perfectly. While Max kept his dark hair cut military short, Ryan's dark hair was a shaggy mess framing a set of sexy eyes. They would drive women nuts, and to Mandy's delight, they were more than happy to accommodate her. If there was another person with access to a number of different models, she was willing to bet money none of them were as sexy as the ones she'd managed to land.

"Just tell us what you need and we're your men."

Ryan's teasing, upbeat personality kept her smiling, and she immediately felt at ease. "Get naked and act natural," she said, somehow managing to keep a straight face.

Max groaned. "Great. Now there's two of them. Don't give him permission, Mandy. We'll never get his clothes back on."

"Fine," she huffed, breaking out her best pout. "You will have to take your shirts off, though." Max flashed a flirtatious glance her way that left her blushing as he stripped his shirt off. Oddly, she knew he didn't mean it. Some people were overtly more sexual than others were. It was more of a vibe he owned. It was as if he couldn't help himself. Of course, the knowledge did nothing to stop her face from burning every time he turned it in her direction. The third time blood flooded her cheeks, she felt Knox's heat pressing into her back. Her heart slammed against her chest at the contact. He was everywhere. Overwhelming. Unmovable.

"He's not for you." His breath fanned across her neck as the whispered warning rang in her ears. The bite in his tone rolled over her skin. As he strode away, she watched the smooth movement of his body. Untamed. The word floated through her mind and she couldn't let it go. He was a predator. Each time he was near, a shot of adrenaline pumped through her veins when she survived the encounter. One day, she wouldn't.

After a few posed shots, Mandy focused on the action. "I'd love to get as many pictures as I can, if you want to take turns sparring. I'm not picky. However the three of you choose to pair up is fine with me."

Knox gave her a sharp nod, and Ryan came over to stand at her side on the edge of the mat. Squaring off, Max and Knox circled one another. Staring down at the digital screen, Mandy zoomed in on Knox and her chest tightened even as she continued snapping pictures.

"Better Max than me," Ryan said, startling her with his tight tone.

Keeping her focus on her task, Mandy tried to keep the curiosity from showing in her voice. "Scared of getting your ass handed to you, huh?" she teased.

"An ass-kicking I can handle. I have

no desire to die. Underground fighters train to compete with only one rule in mind. To the death. I mean, judging by Knox's lifestyle, the money is good, but it takes a certain mentality to go into every match to kill or be killed."

Mandy could hear her heart pounding in her ears. Her gaze slid over his body with a new eye as she searched for any truth to Ryan's claim. The light glimmered off the silver rings in his nipples. Sleek muscles flexed and rolled as he poised for any opening. There wasn't a hint of emotion on his face when he found one and took Max down to the mat. All the deep scars and bruises covering his body made themselves known in light of the new insight. Appearing content with a simple submission, Knox helped an unscathed Max to his feet.

"Oh good. He didn't kill him. I am a

bit attached to him, after all."

Knox looked in their direction at Ryan's words. Raw sensuality dripped from his pores. His eyes darkened with lust. Electricity charged the air between them. Excitement pounded through Mandy. Her nipples ached and a tingle began at the base of her spine.

Ryan cleared his throat. "Whoa," he muttered under his breath. "He's going to do such naughty things to you and I want details," he sang as he walked away, heading in Max's direction. Tearing her eyes away from the man who was making her feel things she shouldn't, she focused her attention on Max and Ryan instead.

Ryan slid his hand down Max's arm as if checking for injuries. She automatically snapped several pictures, doing her best to block out the sexy fighter who moved to stand behind her again. Ignoring the eyes boring into her back, she switched her camera to replay. As she flipped through the final round of shots, checking for focus issues, she paused on a single image. A chill raced through her. She held the equipment closer, zooming in on the impression.

Knox reached over her shoulder, clicking the trash icon. With the picture deleted, he scrolled over to the next one while she stared transfixed at the scar running from his palm all the way to his elbow. The kind of damage people ended up with after they'd slit their wrists, not in the attention-getting way, in the intent-on-dying way. The camera had not been playing tricks on her mind. "Weakness is a family trait," he said against her ear. "This is a much better shot," he added, dragging Mandy's focus back to the screen. She blinked away tears. Her heart ached as Knox set his chin on her shoulder. "How do I crop this one?"

Not trusting her voice, she silently showed him how to adjust the settings on the camera and use the edit feature. Drawing her closer to his chest, he wrapped his arms around her and held the fragile equipment between his hands. As hard as she tried, she couldn't stop studying the deep line and wondering how she'd never noticed it before. The more she thought about it, the more she recognized he didn't invite her stare. When he was near, her eyes danced away in fear. Not of him but of what he did to her senses. Her skin shouldn't heat the way it did in Knox's presence. She'd had sex with his brother, for heaven's sake.

"Oh yeah. This one turned out awesome. You should make a copy for Max and Ryan." Forcing herself to concentrate on the screen, Mandy took note of how Knox had enlarged the image until only the men's faces were visible. Somehow, she'd managed to capture their unique personalities with perfect clarity.

A smile tugged at the corners of her mouth as she recognized what Knox meant for her to see. "Oh. They are in love," she said quietly, and a deep, silky chuckle slipped past his lips at her reaction. The sound went straight to her core, dampening her panties. Turning her head, she inspected the lines of his face.

"Thank you."

His eyes flickered in her direction at the words before skittering away uncomfortably. He didn't shift away, even after transferring the camera back to her hands, and his heat seeped through her thin shirt.

"No thanks needed. It cost me nothing to help out."

"You spent time and energy on me, that's something, and it means more than you could ever know."

Discomfort rolled off him in waves. Mandy stepped out of his embrace, sparing him from dredging up a response. Donning the same overly bright smile she used to get through a day of waiting on tables, Mandy turned the screen so Ryan and Max could see it. "This is my favorite."

* * * * *

The roar of the crowd muted inside Knox's head. His focus locked on his opponent. Another weekend filled with back-to-back brutal no-holds-barred matches. It was second nature, and most likely didn't say good things about him. The two ribs that were probably broken whispered he was an idiot to keep this shit up. Sometimes it was the little guys who snuck one in on him. It wouldn't happen again. The smug look on his opponent's face since landing the nasty kick to Knox's side had to go. An opening appeared. His knuckles cracked against the dude's jaw with enough force to shake the bones in his elbow. Since it already hurt, Knox twisted at the waist and swiped the same elbow across the skinny fighter's temple. He went down hard. Facedown and out for the count.

"Stupid bastard," Jimmy spat the moment Knox reached the edge of the mat. "You have at least fifty pounds on him. What the hell was he thinking?"

"Nothing now," Knox answered without an ounce of shame. The sharp pang in his side carried away any remorse and ratcheted up his temper. "If he can't take the punishment, then he should get out while he can."

Jimmy gave him a sharp nod. "Yep. I can't argue your logic."

There wasn't any back-slapping or congratulations in his world. People came to see blood and win money. That was it. If he came out on top, then he was golden and the crowd loved him. If he lost, then they were likely to do anything. Nobody enjoyed losing a bet. Luckily, he won nine out of ten times. His vicious nature was widely known. If someone was crazy enough to place their money against him, they weren't usually stupid enough to lose their life by confronting him over it afterward.

With his bag packed and money in hand—minus Jimmy's cut, of course—Knox headed for the back door. Dodging all the weirdoes who got hooked on fighters and the people who were just straight-up weird for no particular reason was always the fun part of escaping the warehouse. Two steps from the door, Knox caught a glimpse of Rhys. A willowy blonde hung on his arm. Knox's heart slammed against his chest. With a dip of his chin, Rhys acknowledged him and the girl turned her head in his direction. It wasn't Mandy. The relief washing over him caused the room to spin, until the fury set in. This goddamn bastard had really shown up to his fight with another woman, even after their chat. He couldn't fucking believe it. If Mandy experienced even an ounce of the anger Knox was feeling each time Rhys had done this to her, he couldn't understand why she hadn't killed him. She owned her rage, for real she did.

Rhys took a few steps in his direction, all smiles like the big-ass douche he was. When he caught sight of Knox's stare, he must've understood what Knox wasn't bothering to hide. His steps faltered. For a moment, an expression of complete dejection settled across his features, and Knox felt like shit. What was he supposed to do? Damned if his loyalties weren't split right down the middle. The moment of floundering cost him an escape. Rhys closed the distance between them.

"Did you win?"

"Don't I always?"

The blonde tittered. He hated her. It wasn't her fault, but it didn't matter. Knox had never been accused of having a reasonable nature, and he didn't feel moved to start tonight.

"What brings you by, little brother?"

Rhys' most charming smile snapped into place. "I was bringing Peggy here."

"Penny," she said, interrupting him.

129

A look of confusion passed over Rhys' face. "Isn't that what I said?"

She tittered again. "It's so loud in here. Maybe you did."

Knox added weakness to her list of transgressions.

"Anyhow, I was bringing Peggy to see your match, but we were late on account of, um, some stuff."

It was too much. It really was. "Huh. Sorry you missed it."

The girl set her hand on Knox's arm and he pulled away from her touch. "I-I. Sorry," she stammered. Well, that was it. She was a personal space invader. He hated her times three.

"If you're looking to see a fight, you should convince Rhys to sign up," Jimmy said, cutting into the conversation.

A smile lit her face, and she used it against Rhys. "Oh could you?"

The hopeful note in her voice almost made Knox laugh. It would be hard for his egotistical brother to turn down anything now. In an attempt to save him, Knox elbowed Jimmy and lowered his voice for only him to hear. "He can't fight here, Jimmy. They'll slaughter him."

Jimmy being Jimmy, he couldn't take a hint. "You should challenge him. There's lots of big bets on a brother versus brother battle. You could make a ton of money."

"How much are we talking about here?" Rhys asked, his attention officially snagged. Knox groaned but Jimmy took a good look at the crowd surrounding them.

"It's a huge showing tonight, so I'd say around eight thousand to the winner."

The amount sounded a bit familiar and a wicked smile pulled at his lips. "You know, eight grand reminds me of a certain bill that needs paying."

Never one to back down from an open taunt, Rhys returned the evil grin. "Here are the terms of my surrender: I win, and I'll pay off the monstrous hospital bill. If you win, you pay it off."

A hint of pride in his brother returned, and Knox motioned for Jimmy to make it happen. "Either way, Mandy wins, so I'm in."

"It looks like a new challenge has been issued, folks. Get your wallets out and place your wagers. Our own Knox Collier will be up against his brother Rhys. They are well matched in size and training. This'll be an entertaining one to watch. Not to mention high odds mean big payouts, so get your picks in before it begins."

The announcements continued for fifteen more minutes, giving the crowd time to spend their hard-earned money while Rhys and Knox changed clothes and had their tape signed off on by an official. Luckily, they were close enough in size and weight so Rhys was able to borrow some of Knox's clothes. It was a rush job if Knox had ever seen one, but as far as he was concerned, Mandy deserved it.

The black wire cage nearly shook with the excitement rolling through the building. Stone-faced, Rhys appeared steady and Knox dipped his chin in approval. When the bell rang, it didn't matter who stood across from him, Knox went in hard. Sweeping low, he took out his legs and Rhys hit the mat. Without giving him a chance to recover and cupping his fist for more impact, Knox drove his elbow into Rhys' cheekbone before springing back to his feet. The horde of onlookers roared their approval as blood dripped from the open cut beneath Rhys' eye.

One for Mandy. Rolling back onto his feet, Rhys shook off the blow. Faking to the left, he landed a right jab to Knox's injured ribs, but he paid for it for the close contact and pain he inflicted when Knox took advantage of the move by head-butting him across the bridge of the nose. A second one for good measure.

"Goddamn it, Rhys. Remember where you are. No rules. No mercy!" The trainer in Jimmy showed itself as he emphasized his rant by banging on the cage.

Taking the advice to heart and ignoring the blood that was now gushing, Rhys tackled Knox. The broken bones in Knox's side screamed in protest, stealing the air from his lungs. A moment of darkness surrounded his vision, and Knox wondered if he might lose. Then he heard it. The blonde chick giggled. Oh. Hell no. Rhys made the mistake of only pinning his upper body. Bracing his feet, Knox pushed off before snagging Rhys' body with his legs and flipping him over. The change in momentum allowed him to pin him to mat. Rhys put up a good fight but a forearm to the windpipe had him tapping out. In a show of respect he never offered anyone else, Knox helped Rhys to his feet before slapping him on the back.

"I'm damn proud of you for showing up, but you have too much heart for this place." Rhys swiped at the blood on his face as they left the ring. The fire racing down one side of Knox's body forced him to add, "Although aiming for the cracked ribs was a genius move."

Rhys halted mid-step and his panicked gaze shot to Knox's midsection. "Aim for—you should have told me ahead of time. Holy shit. I could have punctured one of your lungs. What the hell is wrong with you, Knox?"

He should have known. "See? Too much heart for this place." Squeezing his shoulder, he steered Rhys toward the locker room. "Come on. If I pass out from the pain, I'm liable to wake up in some creeper's basement."

At Rhys' insistence, Knox let Jimmy drive him home, but he flat-out refused to go to the hospital. He had survived worse. The only way he would agree to leave his truck behind was upon Rhys' promise he would make sure it he had it back in his driveway before morning.

"Huh. That's a nifty trick." Knox silently agreed with Jimmy's assessment as he eyed the Sierra parked in its usual spot. How Rhys had managed to get the truck home before him was a mystery. "Want to see an even better trick?" Jimmy asked, holding up a cocktail napkin with scribbling across it. "I got Penny's number."

It hurt to laugh. "At least you remember her name." Moving slowly, he slid from the SUV, grunting his thanks as he went. The quiet, upscale neighborhood had gone to bed hours earlier. Only a few lights lit the windows on the street. The tan stone walls of his house stood out in the dark even after Jimmy's headlights disappeared. Punching in his security code to disengage the lock on his front door, Knox slipped inside, closing off the world with the snap of his front door. Silence engulfed him. He'd forgotten to leave a light on...again. The cherry dining room table caught his gym bag when he tossed it. Veering to the left, he dipped inside the first open doorway straight into his bedroom. Bypassing the king-sized bed, he kept his focus locked on his goal. The shower called his name. As soon as he crossed the threshold, a motion sensor switched on the overhead light. Knox flinched against the sudden assault on his senses.

He dumped the contents from his pockets onto the gray marble vanity. The cellphone moved of its own accord, taking him by surprise. In his exhaustion, it took him a moment to understand an incoming text was vibrating his phone across the counter. Bracing his elbows against the cool surface, he swiped his finger across the face and read the message.

It occurs to me you don't have my number, so here I am. Please take advantage of the new knowledge. I know my gratitude makes you uncomfortable, but you can enjoy it while I'm not looking. Thank you for everything you've done for me. There's no way I can repay you.

{{HUGS}} That's all I have but I hope it counts for something—Mandy.

He could hear her voice. Feel her hug. The temptation to jump in his truck and go to her was unbearable. To keep himself from doing anything stupid, he stripped. The bruises would keep him from storming her door even if being arrested for indecent exposure didn't. Turning the water as hot as it would go, he stepped into the center of it. Steady, pulsating streams from five different showerheads hit him all at once. He bit out a hiss. In an attempt to escape the pain, he pictured Mandy. The look in her eyes as she stared at his chest. Blood rushed to his groin and his cock lengthened. Dropping his chin to his chest, Knox stared down at the erection that was too stupid to realize she would never want him in such a way. The sensation of her hair brushing his cheek as he enlarged a picture on her camera came rushing back to him. Even her sweet smell seemed to linger in the steam. His hand slid down his stomach. She'd turned her head until her lips were mere inches from his. It was torture. He'd wanted to claim the sexy mouth as his own. His fingers slipped lower until he gave into the inevitable by palming his shaft. Did she moan when she found release? With her pussy in his mouth, he would ensure it.

The base of his spine itched as he pumped his fist. In his mind it was Mandy's inner muscles squeezing him. His breathing hitched up and his eyes fell closed. He wanted to fuck her. Hard. Until they both collapsed from exhaustion. A gasp rose in his throat and his balls drew up tight. Hot semen shot out in a stream as an orgasm rolled through him. Bracing his weight against the wall, Knox fought to breathe. His hands shook. Fear like he'd never known welled inside him. Somewhere along the way, Mandy had become necessary to him, and he understood what Drew had been trying to tell him. There was no low he wouldn't stoop to in order to have her, and his scruples were pretty damn non-existent already.

Chapter Four

Knox didn't come for coffee, not the next day nor the day after that. She watched for him each morning only to end up disappointed. By the time an entire week passed, she felt deflated. In hopes of achieving the perfect prints, Mandy had dropped her memory card off with a professional for enlargement after the photo shoot. She added an extra order for Max and Ryan as Knox had suggested. When the time—finally—rolled around to pick them up, she carefully tucked the packages in her messenger bag and headed straight for Grid Iron. If Knox wouldn't come to her, then she would go to him. She missed him and she wasn't above forcing her way into his life.

The last time she'd visited the fitness center, she'd been with Knox. She half-expected they'd give her hard time at the door and refuse to allow her entrance. To her surprise, the same curvy brunette was working the desk, and she waved Mandy inside with a smile. "You have perfect timing. The guys are between classes."

The cheerful woman looked vaguely familiar. Mandy had been too nervous about the photo shoot the last time they'd met to notice, but now she couldn't shake the feeling. Unable to stop herself, she asked, "Have we met someplace other than here before?"

A line formed between the girl's brows and she scrunched her face up in thought. She truly was adorable. The thought caused Mandy to smile. "I don't think so," she answered after a moment.

Mandy shook her head. "Who

knows? Maybe it's just one of those things. There is something familiar about you. I've probably waited on you at Black River once or something similar."

"People do tell me I look a lot like my brother, so maybe that's it."

"Who's your brother?" Mandy asked, immediately curious.

"Ryan. I'm Kerry Crawford," she added, holding her hand out for Mandy to shake. Mandy eyed Kerry's dimples and green eyes framed by unnaturally long lashes.

"Oh, I see it now!" She accepted Kerry's hand before adding, "I'm Mandy Everett, in case I didn't say so the other day. Wow, it seems like everyone is related."

"Eh," Kerry said, waving off Mandy's words. "It's the way of the world. Somebody in your family hooks you up with a job, and then you never leave because you're comfortable. You know how it is."

Mandy pulled a face. "Unfortunately, yes. I've been at Black River for an eternity. Hopefully, with your brother's help, I'll be out of there soon," she said, tapping her messenger bag. The phone rang and Kerry tossed a glance in its direction.

"The guys are in the same room as last time. I guess I'd better act like I work here."

With a final wave over her shoulder, Mandy wove her way through the stationary bikes and weight machines until she reached the back of the club. The door stood partially open. Peeking in, she spotted Max and Ryan on the opposite side of the room with their heads together and checking out something on Ryan's phone. Hesitant to disturb them, she paused in the doorway. After a moment of simply observing them together, she wished she'd brought her camera. They had something she wanted to capture and freeze in time. She was almost jealous. Max pushed the phone aside and touched his lips to Ryan's, making Mandy a bit ashamed of her intrusion.

Rapping her knuckles on the wood of the door, she announced her presence. Max pressed closer to Ryan for a second before slowly pulling away and turning in her direction. A smile lit Ryan's face when he spied her lingering inside the entryway.

"Hey, Mandy. We were wondering when we'd be hearing from you."

Stepping into the room, Mandy did her best to hide a blush as Max flashed a grin her way. Instead, she concentrated on tugging the thinner of the two envelopes out of her bag. "I've brought you a gift," she explained, waving it at them. "I hoped Knox would be hanging around here somewhere as well, but I didn't see him out there."

"He won't be here today."

Something in Max's tone set off warning bells in her mind. "Is everything okay?"

"It's Sunday," both men said simultaneously as if it should explain everything.

"Okay," she drawled. Giving up on gaining a straight answer, she pried open the seal on the envelope. They took turns passing the pictures around. The open happiness on their faces reminded her of why she loved photography. Pictures were proof of existence. They froze a moment out of time and held memories for safekeeping. The itch to share the moment with Knox was making her skin crawl. Her mind raced for a way to make it happen.

When the idea came, it seemed almost too simple, and she had to stop herself from rushing from the room. She barely understood a word of the conversation. Making her excuses, she left the men to enjoy the prints while she ducked out. Halfway to the front desk, she dug through her purse, making a huge show of it until she reached Kerry's side.

Donning her best overly frazzled expression, she set her bag on the counter. "I'm supposed to mail a set of these prints to Knox, but I can't find where I wrote down his address," she explained, throwing as much exasperation as she could into her tone. "I sort of hoped he'd be here today so I could hand it to him personally and not look like an idiot for losing it. I swear I cannot keep up with anything."

"Oh. Let me look it up for you,"

Kerry offered. Tearing off a sticky note, she added, "Knox never comes in on Sunday since he's usually too sore after the weekend fight schedule, and I understand your dilemma. My purse is like a black hole. Once something goes in, it's sucked into oblivion. If you haven't found it by now you never will." After a few quick clicks on the computer, Kerry jotted down Knox's address and handed it over.

Mandy clutched it to her chest. "You're a lifesaver. Thank you so much."

"You're very welcome. We girls have to stick together."

* * * * *

The banging on his front door wouldn't let up. Giving in, Knox dragged a pair of jeans up his legs, but he couldn't dredge up the energy to button them. He threw open the door prepared to shove whatever vacuum he was about to get sold up someone's ass.

149

Mandy shifted nervously under his black scowl, and he immediately locked down his emotions to keep from scaring her.

"Um," she stammered, making him feel like shit.

He took a step back. "Sorry. I was in the shower. Come on in." Even though she still looked unsure of her welcome, she stepped past him and he inhaled her scent into his lungs. Goddamn, everything about her made him want to own her.

"Oh. Wow. Your house is gorgeous." Without waiting for a response, she added, "I picked up the photos today. I was hoping you'd help me pick out the best ones for my portfolio." She crinkled her nose in a way that did something to his chest. "It's ridiculous, but I'm my own worst critic. If I try to do this alone, I'll never be able to pick, and it will end in tears."

Not giving him time to answer, she

kicked off her flip-flops and headed for the kitchen table. She set a huge brown leather bag on top and dug around inside. The tiny cotton shorts showcasing her long legs, and the form-fitting low-cut V-neck t-shirt that flashed a bit of cleavage with every move she made, almost had him offering to let her have the house. She pulled out an overstuffed envelope from inside the bag, and broke the seal. The glossy photos slid into a stack on the table. He inched closer to get a better look.

She eyed his bare torso with interest for a moment before shaking her head. "It's always your poor ribs." Waving it off, she continued as if it didn't matter, and he couldn't help the smile pulling at his lips. "I want to divide the pictures up into four piles. One for action shots, one for body shots, one for eyes, and one for images that aren't so good. Are you going to help?"

It took him a moment to absorb the truth, she accepted him as he was. There wouldn't be any lectures over his lifestyle. He would never have any need to hide anything from her. She was perfect, and he hadn't heard a word she said.

"Um, sure," he agreed in an attempt to show her the same respect. It didn't really matter what she'd asked, anyhow. He was up for anything. "Just tell me what you need me to do."

"Take these." She split the stack into two parts before handing him half. "Get started on separating them into piles and then we'll switch. We'll go through each other's choices and cull it that way." After a few minutes of watching her, he got the idea of what she expected. To him, all the photos were amazing. He didn't add anything to the not-so-good stack because they didn't deserve to be there.

"You'll be stuck with me all day at this rate. We won't get anywhere if you don't make some cuts over there," she said on a laugh.

"Maybe I like keeping you to myself." When Mandy kept her head down and didn't respond to his open flirtation, he added, "I'm sorry. I guess I suck at this because they're all great. I don't want to get rid of any of them. What did you choose?" Leaning over the edge of the table, he checked out her four piles and spotted one facedown picture. He flipped it over. An image of Rhys sprawled across Mandy's couch stared out at Knox. Her hand shot out as if hoping to spare him from the sight. She hesitated over the photo before quickly flipping it over again. He hated that she loved him. A spike of jealousy slammed into him. Red coated his vision. His body pressed against hers as he boxed her in against the table. Knox didn't recall moving. One moment, he'd been standing a few feet away. The next, he was staring down at her. With Mandy trapped, he shifted his hands to her hips. Her breathing was fast and hard. She kept her gaze glued to his chest, but it was too late. He knew what she was hiding. She couldn't conceal her body's reactions. Nostrils flared, Knox absorbed the sight of Mandy's beaded nipples showing through her shirt.

"Look at me," he demanded.

Doing as he bade, she slowly lifted her chin. Pupils dilated with a deep flush across her cheekbones, Mandy was the perfect picture of sexual longing. His lips curled into a knowing grin.

"I told you not to trust me," he reminded her in his most mocking tone.

Need crawled at his spine. The nights he'd lain awake, fantasizing about touching her, caused his grip to tighten possessively at her waist.

"Make me," she taunted, recklessly. A menacing chuckle fell from his lips as he lowered his head to the column of her throat. He curled his fingers around the hem of her shirt. His knuckles scraped along her skin as he inched the material up. Chill bumps rose where his breath fanned across her neck when he spoke.

"You shouldn't provoke someone like me. I'm no one's gentle lover." To emphasize his words, he sank his teeth into the soft flesh that was teasing him. Her hands fluttered to his waist, but he forced them upward as he yanked the shirt over her head, exposing her lacy bra for his perusal. His cock lengthened and wept. He was addicted.

Succumbing to his desire, he unhooked the scrap of material and allowed it to slip to the floor. Cupping her breast, he swiped his thumb over one of her nipples. A cry broke past her lips and her eyes fell closed.

He gave her a tiny shake. "No. You will keep your eyes open for this. I refuse to have you think of anyone except for me." Sweeping his hands down her sides, Knox pushed her shorts down a couple of inches. "When your pussy is flooding my mouth, it will be my name on your lips."

When her lids lifted, her eyes flashed with hunger, which merely fed his craving. Lust tinged her voice as she whispered, "I've imagined you kissing me a thousand times. Make it real."

Left with no other choice, Knox pulled her in and his lips collided with hers. He teased her mouth open with the tip of his tongue. Because he couldn't not taste her. It was sinful delight. The flavor of sweet innocence exploded across his taste buds, causing his cock to twitch. A dark yearning to corrupt her roared through him when her tongue shyly returned his caress. Her admission had sealed her fate.

Knox shoved both hands down the back of her pants, taking hold of Mandy's bare ass and hauling her forward. The firm round globes fit perfectly in his hands. He ground her pelvis against his erection, making sure she understood there was no backing down. Her moan vibrated around his tongue and his cock twitched.

Power surged through him at the skin-on-skin contact. His dick leaked with the first tentative touch of her fingers on his chest. When her nails scraped over the silver rings in his nipples, he jerked away. She made him want more than he should, and this wasn't about him.

A flash of hurt crossed over her features. He wanted to wash it away. Going down onto his knees, he took her shorts and panties with him as he went. Mandy gasped. Grasping the edge of the table behind her, she almost appeared to be clinging to it for support. He hid a grin. Off balance was exactly where he wanted her.

"Let me have these," he demanded, forcing her to step out of the remainder of her clothing. Tossing it aside, he focused on his prize. Knox didn't allow her enough time to think. Under normal circumstances, she was too smart to let someone like him touch her. With one hand pressing against her stomach, he pushed her into the table to keep her from falling as he snagged her ankle and hooked her leg over his shoulder. Her hairless pussy glistened with moisture, and water flooded his mouth. The hunger to swallow her juices caused fire to lash at his throat.

"Knox."

His name falling from her lips was his undoing. His heart slammed against his chest as he slid his tongue along her slit, parting her pussy lips. He drew her scent into his lungs. Sexy. Enchanting. His. She pumped her hips against his mouth as he found her tiny nub, taking it between his teeth. He wanted her to claim her pleasure. Slipping a finger inside her channel, Knox groaned as her tight, wet heat clenched around it. The picture of her doing the same thing to his cock nearly caused him to come inside his jeans.

Pushing aside his need, he used her moisture against her, trailing a line from her opening to her ass. She sucked in a deep gasp as he teased the sensitive nerves around her puckered strawberry at the same time as he circled her clit with his tongue. He pressed against the tight ring of muscles keeping him out. Mandy grasped his shoulders and dug her nails deep into his skin. A deep, silky chuckle fell from his lips as he realized she'd never had anyone touch her like this.

Tilting her hips, he slid his tongue past her opening, teasing the spot between her cunt and anus before moving to her strawberry, leaving it soaked with his saliva.

"Knox, please?"

Her plea only made him more determined. Without giving her a chance to protest, he claimed her clit, sucking hard upon it as he drove two fingers inside her ass. Liquid heat flooded his mouth as her body pulled greedily at his fingers. Her channel pulsed. Her cries filled his ears, driving something primal inside him. He didn't let up. Stabbing his tongue inside her cunt, he growled as she tightened around it. With one last pump of his fingers, he slipped them out before she came down from her high.

Knox turned his head and pressed his face against her inner thigh. Blood rushed in his ears, making it hard for him to hear as he called upon every ounce of his restraint. When he was sure he could do so without causing permanent damage, he stumbled to his feet. Mandy's lips parted as she gasped for air. Pushing her hair away from her face, Knox held her gaze. The light-blue irises staring back at him were the center of an obsession he couldn't let go. He almost feared himself in that moment. Holding her face between his hands, he fed his addiction.

"If you have an ounce of good sense, you will stay away from me." He didn't mean to say it. The necessity to caution her outweighed the dark urges clawing at his skin.

"Why do you keep warning me away?"

Instead of answering, Knox slammed his mouth down on hers, cutting off any more questions. She opened for him without any encouragement. He growled at her easy acquiescence and he tried to push her by sucking on her tongue before biting at her lips. Instead of rejecting him, she moaned. At the sound, he turned his head away. With his arms wrapped around her waist, he pressed his lips to her shoulder. He could not do this if she didn't understand what she was getting in him.

*

"I watch you." Mandy held her breath at Knox's whispered confession. He spoke against her skin, and she was almost scared he wouldn't continue. "When you're not looking," he added. "You don't notice me, but I'm there. It's not right for me to want you. I'm not a good person."

His arms fell away and he dropped his gaze to the floor as he took a step back. Blindly, Mandy reached for him. Panic over the loss of him had her closing the distance he created. She could feel his emotions closing down. She couldn't stand it.

"I see you," she blurted out, calling him back to her. "At eight fifteen every morning, you step through the door of Black River. I know the precise moment you arrive and every movement you make while you are there. On the days I work a double, you're back at two, but you don't stay as long. It's been exactly twenty-two days since the last time—"

Knox kissed her, cutting off her speech. Delicious. The word continued filling her mind at his flavor. Smooth strokes flowed across her tongue. Intoxicating her. Enticing her. Making her forget. Her feet left the floor as Knox swept her into his arms.

She automatically clutched at his neck to keep her balance.

"I only want to hold you, okay?" he said as he passed through an open doorway to their left. The smell of his cologne filled the air. She caught a flash of dark curtains, but she couldn't look away from the set lines of his face. Even as her back touched the mattress of what had to be his bed, she didn't turn away.

"Why?"

"I don't know," he said, answering her question honestly. "I just need to have your skin against mine."

"What if I want more?"

With one knee braced on the mattress, Knox stopped dead at her question. His expression never changed but his eyes flashed with fire. "Then you should take whatever you like."

With his consent hanging in the air, Mandy sprang into action before she could chicken out. Hooking his knee with her heel and curling her fingers around his wrist, she used his weight against him. With a sharp tug, she sent him tumbling. Without giving him a chance to recover from his shock, Mandy pushed him onto his back. Knox's surprised bark of laughter died on a moan when her lips closed around his nipple. She tugged at the ring between her teeth. The taste of man and metal filled her mouth as his wild scent tickled her nostrils.

He lifted his weight to help her along

as she shoved at the waistband of his jeans. She gently scraped at his skin with her fingernails as she peeled the material down his legs. It was his eyes. She'd never felt more desirable or powerful in her life than when he was looking at her.

As she crawled back up his body, Mandy paused to trace a white scar across his thigh with her tongue. His muscles jumped and she smiled against his skin. His dark- blue boxer briefs were soaked with pre-cum, proving how turned on he was.

"You're killing me, Mandy."

"We can't have that," she said with a wicked smile as she dragged the underwear over his hips as well. His engorged cock swelled farther beneath her gaze. Tracing the slit at the tip, she smeared his juices around the crown, licking her lips.

His cock jerked and his hips left the

bed in his attempt to move closer to her. "Fuck." The curse sounded like it came from his soul. Sweat pooled at the base of her spine as she fought for restraint. She held his erection steady. His gaze homed in on her as she opened her lips around his shaft. Hot liquid flooded her pussy at the taste of masculine salt upon her tongue.

The nape of her neck stung as Knox gripped her hair but he released her just as quickly. With a swirl of her tongue around his crown, she allowed him to slip from her mouth. "Don't treat me like glass," she warned before closing her mouth around his cock and hollowing out her cheeks.

With an accusing pull on her roots, Knox growled. "Then don't fucking tease me." He punctuated his words by grinding his hips against her mouth. Mandy loosened her jaw before taking him to the back of her throat. The guttural sounds he made as she swallowed him caused her to increase her pace. Her channel pulsed with the desire to have him filling her. She wanted to feel him driving inside her, but she was intent on making him cry her name. Saliva coated her fingers at his root. She rolled his balls between the fingers of her other hand before slipping lower. It was a calculated risk.

She'd loved everything he'd done to her and she could only hope he would have the same reaction. Tracing the line from his sac to his ass, she played upon those sensitive nerve endings, taking cues from his reactions to her touch. Knox drew his knee up, giving her more room to move, and she purred with ecstasy. Free rein over his body was more than any woman could dream of having. She shaped his dick with her tongue while circling his asshole with her finger, unsure of how far her bravery went.

It turned out not to matter. With a sharp tug, Knox drew her up his body until her wet cunt was straddling his torso. His eyes looked feverish and his words came out sounding ravaged. "Grab a condom out of that drawer to your left. I want to be inside you when I come."

Doing as he bade, Mandy opened the drawer and condom with shaking hands. Her fingers fumbled as she helped him suit up. He snagged her hips, holding her in place. "This isn't a one-time thing. I don't share. Do you understand me?"

Her heart slammed against her chest with such force Mandy thought she might die. "Yes," she whispered past dry lips.

He rocked upward, sliding his cock into her opening slightly before withdrawing. "Tell me you belong to me," he demanded. "I need to know you're mine." The desperation in his gaze left her breathless.

Her eyes burned and her nose prickled even as her overly sensitized nub begged for his attention. "I'm yours." Before the echo of her promise died away and in one swift motion, Mandy found herself pinned beneath two-hundred-plus pounds of turned on male. He crushed the air from her lungs as he surged inside her. Her channel stretched wide to accommodate him. Oxygen no longer mattered to her. Animalistic desire clawed at her skin and she locked her inner muscles around his shaft in an attempt to keep him from withdrawing.

Knox's teeth scraped the column of her throat while she dug her heels into the mattress, pressing closer to him. "Please?" She didn't care that she was begging. "I hurt." Hanging on the edge of orgasm, she had no pride left. Even as his dick pumped inside her, Knox reached between them and pressed against her clit with his thumb, forcing her to take her pleasure. Demanding lips met hers and excitement pounded through her. Electric twinges singed her nerve endings as she rubbed herself against his touch. Her focus locked on the tingling between her legs as her muscles tensed in anticipation. Cupping his ass, Mandy dug her fingernails into his skin as the first spasm rocketed through her. His name tore from her throat and his teeth sank into her shoulder, ratcheting up the intensity of the orgasm tearing through her.

A strangled cry left him as he drove forward one last time. The assault on her senses left her shredded. She clutched him tighter to her chest when his weight landed on her. Heated lips touched her cheek, stealing her soul. She understood something better in that moment than ever before. Breathing was overrated.

*

With one arm thrown over Mandy's chest, Knox kept her pinned to the bed. After cleaning up his mess, he'd spent several minutes enjoying the feel of having her tucked against him. He thought she'd fallen asleep until her fingertips slid down the inside of his forearm, sketching his scar. For some reason he couldn't explain, he needed her to know he wasn't weak-natured. "It was a long time ago."

She jumped in surprise and her gaze shot to his. "I thought you were sleeping."

At her statement, he smiled in spite

of himself. "I was just thinking the same thing about you." He traced the outline of her cheek with his eyes. "You're so damn gorgeous."

"Thank you," she responded, sounding prim. "You're pretty damn hot yourself." With a grumble of laughter, Knox came up onto his elbow and hovered over her.

Following the motion with his gaze, he trailed his thumb over her bottom lip. The tip of her tongue shot out, swiping along its pad before disappearing again. Unable to do otherwise, Knox captured her mouth with his. Lips parted, neither of them moved to deepen the kiss. It was an exchanging of breath and more intimate than anything they'd done thus far.

He glided his hand down her body and grasped her hip before closing his teeth around her bottom lip. When her hands fluttered at his back, something shifted in his chest. The roar of possessiveness he'd felt before claiming her body paled in comparison to the beast currently rising inside him. In that moment, he recognized something important. He would kill anyone who attempted to take her from him.

The arousal always simmering under his skin when she was near fired to life. Without any real plan of doing so, he rolled until she was trapped underneath him. His hand slipped between their bodies as his tongue fought hers for dominance. Slickened, wet folds met his touch, making his cock ache, dripping. Palming himself, Knox teased her sensitized nub with his crown. It was pure torture. Her kiss became demanding. The brush of her inner thighs against his hips drove him insane. Hot liquid from her pussy coated his needy dick. Her tight opening beckoned him. The tip of his cock slipped inside her channel before sliding out again. Knox groaned as he tore his mouth away.

"Fucking condom. I forgot." The dazed look in her eyes combined with her body's reaction to his touch almost caused him to forget again. "This has never happened to me before," he said, pleading for her to understand what she did to him.

"I'm on the pill," she said misunderstanding his words. "I have been ever since..." Her face became hard as she trailed off and he recognized himself in her expression. Life pissed her off. It didn't beat her down. It made her mad as hell, just as it did him. He wanted to fix it. He needed her whole. Without warning, he surged forward. She gasped when he was fully seated inside her, but the anger left her face. With lust clawing at his spine, he still managed to hold her gaze as he promised her the world. "I won't ever let you hurt again."

* * * * *

Mandy knew there was a special place in hell for people who brought donuts and coffee into a fitness center. Of course, she still did. Kerry's face lit up at the sight of her. Shaking the box in her hand, Mandy sang, "I have something for you."

"Ooh," Kerry sighed as she stretched for the box, but at the last second Mandy held it out of her reach.

"This is a bribe so you won't tell Knox you heard the news first." Kerry's face brightened even more. "You got the job."

"I got the job!" Mandy screamed. Kerry jumped up and down squealing. Inside, Mandy was doing the same girlie dance. In her four-inch heels, she didn't dare attempt it. Kerry rescued the coffee and donuts before giving her a quick hug.

"Sheesh, I feel like a hobbit next you. Good grief. Those heels must put you well over six feet."

Mandy waved off her words. "Please, girl. I've always wished I was short and curvy instead of towering over everyone like some sort of Amazon woman. Try being taller than almost every man you meet. It's a bitch."

Kerry rolled her eyes. "Whatever," she muttered. With a sweeping glance, Kerry checked out Mandy's pencil skirt, which landed mid-thigh, and her thin coral-colored silk shirt. "I assume you're not here to work out."

"Ha! If you ever see me running, you had better look to see who's chasing me. Seriously, I'll probably drop dead at sixty of a heart attack, but I don't like going to the gym. I just wanted to pop by and tell you how it went."

Kerry settled onto the stool behind the check-in counter. "I'm so glad you did. Knox is still here, if you want to go back and share the news."

A giddy feeling rose inside her. "If it's okay, then I'd love to."

"Hell yeah, it's okay," Kerry agreed immediately. "Here. Let me give you this." Opening one of her drawers, Kerry pulled out a card. It reminded Mandy of one of the keycards Black River handed out to hotel guests. After clicking a few keys on the computer, Kerry stuck the card into a square electronic device. It beeped twice. She handed it over. "You'll need this to get into the training center."

Mandy palmed the card with a grateful smile and Kerry stood, once more. "Here's what you're going to do. After you go through this door, instead of turning right, toward the weights and classrooms, as you usually do, you're going to go left." Kerry twisted her hips and mimicked her directions, reminding Mandy of a flight attendant. "There's a long hallway. You'll see the locker rooms on the right hand side of the hall and then it's the next door on the left. Scan the card and you'll be good. Make sure you hang on to it so you'll have access from now on. Plus, if you drive around back, there is a metal staircase that leads straight there, and you can use the pass to unlock the door, but I hope you don't skip out on seeing me," she added with a wink.

"Oh my gosh, Kerry. Thank you. Will you get into trouble for this?"

Kerry scoffed. "Nah. Max owns this place. Well, he does now that his father has passed away. He's been running it for the past few years since his dad's been sick, anyhow, so there wasn't really any change for us. He loves my brother way too much to ever get angry with me. I'm a good employee, but I also do as I please."

Mandy clutched the card to her chest with a surge of gratefulness. "You're amazing."

"Go on," she said with a blush. After a moment, she added. "But really, I know I am."

A roar of laughter rolled through Mandy. "Enjoy your snack and I'll stop by again on my way out."

Kerry waved her away. "Yes. Please go away. I can't eat this in front of your skinny ass."

With a shake of her head, Mandy headed inside. The training area was simple to find with Kerry's directions. Several people paused to eye her as she passed, but she ignored them. The metal door handle turned easily in her hand once she scanned the card. The scent of man and leather assailed her senses as soon as she stepped inside. Back when she'd been a little girl, her father had been a prize-fighter for Black River's Casino division, and the smell caused nostalgia to roll through her. However, boxing was a very different sport from the no-holds-barred-style fights people trained for in places such as these.

Some aspects of the sport were the same. The punching bags and roped-off ring looked similar to the ones her father had used, but she knew from going to Rhys' matches, these men faced-off in wire cages. Her gaze took in two men taking shots at one another inside the ring while several others called out suggestions. The sound of solid punches landing on a bag rang out rhythmically, reverberating off the dark walls. In stark contrast to the brightly lit classrooms, this part of the building seemed almost dingy.

One of the men at the edge of the ring caught sight of her and nudged the man next to him. To her surprise, all activity came to a halt. Pasting on her most luminous smile, Mandy gave them a small wave. "Hey guys. Is Knox around?"

An older gentleman with puffs of white hair and a bright red face gave a sharp nod at her question. "Sure, sugar. Knox, there's some smoking-hot chick asking for you!" She winced at his unexpected bellow. Holding back a laugh, she mouthed "thank you", and his slow wink made her face flush red. She shifted nervously under the men's stares. When Knox finally appeared from the opposite side of the room, a wave of relief rushed over her.

She'd always hated being the center of attention. The urge to begin flashing her keycard while screaming "I have a pass" overcame her.

The picture of Knox crossing the room to her side wiped away her anxiety. He was barefoot, bare-chested and tape covered his knuckles. A pair of workout pants rode low on his hips, allowing the tail of the dragon tattooed on his side to show across his oblique muscles. Her body hummed to life. Every fluid movement he produced reminded her of the way he made love to her. The green of his eyes sharpened when he spotted her. She wondered how she'd ever believed he was detached from the world around him. Knox was an emotional charge on overdrive. Most likely, he felt more than most people ever did. It turned her on.

"Hey babe," he said while snagging

her waist and hauling her against him. As his lips caressed hers, the club roared back to life. "Damn, I needed that." The combination of his confession and kiss left her breathless. "You're taller," he added, dropping his gaze to her feet.

Mandy huffed. "You came from all the way across this big-ass room and you're just now noticing the heels?"

A smile hovered at the corners of his mouth as he answered. "It's your fault. I couldn't tear my eyes away from your face. Actually, I might embarrass myself if these guys get a good enough view of me right now. The way you look at me, damn." His growled curse dampened her panties. She wanted to press closer to feel the proof of his arousal for herself. Somehow, she kept her feet glued to the floor. She forgot why she was there until he called her back. "How did the interview go?"

"I got the job."

Knox threw his arms up. "Woot! She got the job!"

A round of cheers rang out and Mandy blushed hotly. "Has everyone been waiting on the word?" she asked in a stage whisper.

"Have you met Kerry? She tells everything she knows to everyone."

Mandy pressed her lips together in an attempt to hold on to her admission but she couldn't. "I guess I should confess, then. I told her first."

Knox roared with laughter. Mandy wasn't the only who froze to stare at the rare occurrence. While he wiped away a tear of mirth, she studied his luminous smile. "Goddamn, you make me happy," he said while crowding her with his body. "Baby, Kerry would have tackled you in the doorway if you'd tried to get past her without saying anything." She didn't hear a single thing past the "happy" part.

"I make you happy?" She couldn't hide the wonder in her voice.

Cupping her chin, Knox traced her bottom lip with his thumb as he answered. "If I had you alone right now, I'd show you exactly how high you take me, baby."

"Oh, so not alone," she said more as a reminder for herself than anyone. Stepping out of his embrace, she put a bit of distance between them to hang on to her sanity. "I stopped by for another reason," she added, forcing her body to take a breather before she gave everyone a show. She stuffed her keycard into her purse. Pulling out the envelope she'd found in her mailbox earlier in the day, she waved it in his direction. "Someone paid off my hospital bill."

The blank countenance she was accustomed to dealing with fell back into place. "Um, about that." Her eyebrows rose in question when he didn't say anything else. With a heavy sigh, he scrubbed his hands across the back of his head. "I have some connections at the hospital..." He floundered helplessly before groaning like a man doomed. "I gave the bill to Rhys."

She had nothing. Every response she could think up died a fiery death before leaving her lips. With a curse, Knox steered her toward the door. Her feet obeyed while her mind whirled. No matter which path it took, it returned to one thing: Rhys knew. Knox led her out one door and through another. The smell of disinfectant lingered in the air. A row of shelves stocked with paper towels and liquid soap covered one wall. An extra weight bench sat abandoned against another.

"We're in a supply closet," she said absently. It was a ridiculous observation. There was nothing else. No matter how much she probed at the recesses of her brain, she came out empty-handed. "And you're barefoot," she added, but he still waited patiently for her to get back on topic. "Seriously, they store mops in here. There are probably potty germs everywhere."

He ignored her asinine comments. "Let me have it. You have every right to be pissed off at me, but I want you to say it."

"I'm not." She really wasn't. She accepted the truth as the words left her mouth. "I mean, obviously I should have been the one to tell him, but I didn't. It was wrong. It's just, I couldn't." It was easily the worst explanation for her actions on the planet, but Knox still nodded. The understanding etched in the lines of his face made her realize he honestly did get it. Pain ate away at her heart. "He's your brother," she said helplessly.

He turned inside himself. The emotional retreat almost caused her to cry out in loss. His stoic tone did nothing to help matters. "Yes. He is."

"One day, you'll see me as the person who came between the two of you, and you'll look at me wearing the exact expression you are right now." Mandy swallowed hard as she grasped the reality of their situation. "It'll kill me."

"No."

Mandy's drew her brows together. "What do you mean, no?"

He took a step forward, forcing her to retreat, and then another, until her back hit the wall and she couldn't go any farther. His face remained rigid even as he flattened his palms against the wall on either side of her head. "I mean no. You don't get to make me feel alive only to take it away. If you're angry with me, I expect you to say so. If I've done something to hurt you, you're going to fucking tell me, but you do not get—"

She sealed her mouth over his, cutting off the words.

Throwing her bag on the floor, she buried both hands in his hair and held him in place. With one last nip at his bottom lip, she pulled away and stared into his eyes, making sure he understood. "You don't get to shut me out. I don't give a shit which face you show the rest of the world. Everything inside you is mine."

Knox's eyes fell closed as his forehead came to rest against hers. "It wasn't intentional. I swear."

"It's a defense mechanism. I get that." She gave him a tiny shake to make him open his eyes before whispering, "I want to be under your skin the way you're under mine."

"You're way past that point." With a mischievous grin, he added, "This outfit is driving me nuts." The short skirt inched up a notch with his help. When she didn't stop him, he tugged it even higher until there was nothing between her hips and the rough pull of his hand wraps. His fingers curled around the elastic of her thong. "I can wait. Until I have you in bed," he clarified. Even as he made the claim, the silk material slid down her thighs with his help.

"I can't."

With a smirk, he crouched in front of her. The skin beneath her palms felt unnaturally hot as she braced her weight on his shoulders while he lifted one foot and then the other, peeling away her panties. When he stood once more, he stuffed them inside his pocket.

"These are mine for now."

"I'm not sure they're your color, but whatever." Her joke came out sounding breathless. The slick material of her skirt had immediately slid back into place as soon as Knox had let go of it. He remedied the problem by inching it upward again. He stared at her without a hint of his true feelings on his face, except for his eyes. They burned.

Her hands shaped his biceps while her channel throbbed. Gliding her palms down his chest, Mandy didn't stop until she reached the waistband of his pants. She hooked her thumbs around the edges.

"I don't know how to be normal," he confessed.

"I don't want normal. I want you inside me." She set his erection free. Her heartbeat quickened. The silken skin of his shaft called for her touch. His gaze became hooded and his voice harshened when she took him in hand.

"You're already inside me." Swooping in, Knox froze half an inch from her lips even as he urged her hips forward and her knee to his waist. His breath fanned across her cheek. "Do you feel it yet?"

She felt so many things. "What?"

"The truth," he answered quietly. "It has always been you."

Understanding slammed into her at the same time as the blunt head of his cock pushed past her opening. He seized her mouth. Memories flooded her brain. He'd always been hovering at the edge of her life. Patient. Slowly seducing her. Waiting. Undaunted.

"I gave you plenty of chances to get away." He curled his tongue around hers before moaning against her mouth. "Mine now."

She couldn't deny it, nor did she want to. He owned her completely. Her muscles quivered under his sensual destruction. Even her nipples ached for more of him as streaks of pleasure ran through her. With a strength she didn't know she possessed, Mandy turned her face away. "Bench," she suggested, gasping for air. Her feet left the floor as he shifted away from the wall to give her what she wanted. The moment his ass hit the seat, she took control. Scoring his shoulders with her nails, she rocked against him. The direct stimulation of his body against her clit drove her wild. Mandy threw her head back as his teeth scraped along her collarbone and his hips rose to meet her thrusts. His arms kept her locked tight in his grasp while guttural cries ripped from his throat. Her muscles tensed as pleasure coiled in her stomach. The edge of ecstasy beckoned her. Knox swept a hand down her back, squeezing her ass before trailing his fingertips along her crevice. She held her breath. Waiting. His lips moved from her neck to her mouth. His tongue teased her lips while his fingers taunted her with their presence. Pushing his way inside, Knox surged upward, and Mandy moaned as an orgasm tore through her. A strangled noise came from deep inside him as he came.

Even as the haze of lust ebbed, Knox continued pumping his finger inside her ass. She was panting. It was unnaturally loud, but she couldn't stop. Her flesh was inflamed from his touch. Every place their skin met sang with decadence.

His mouth moved to her ear and his lips brushed her lobe with every deep, silky word he spoke. "One day soon, I'll fuck you here." He pressed another finger inside her, stretching her wide. The already sensitive nerve endings sang under his touch. Hot liquid rushed from her pussy, soaking his cock with the proof of their combined pleasure. Raw sexuality dripped from his voice. "Use me, Mandy. Get yourself off on my body. Let me watch."

Turning her head, she met his gaze. His eyes—damn—they stole everything from her. They burned with an overload of lust, leaving her shattered and willing to do anything he wanted. She didn't doubt she would have killed for him if he asked her to in that moment. Making sure his stare followed her movements, Mandy skimmed her hand down her body until she could slide her fingers along her slit. His nostrils flared, sending a shiver of yearning through her. Her clit pulsed as she circled it. A moan slipped past her lips.

"That's it, baby. You're so damn sexy. When I get you in bed I'll lick you clean." The tingle between her legs increased with every word he said. The flush across his cheekbones held her captivated. Everything about Knox was the definition of carnality. "Let me have it," he demanded, and proving he was her body's master, an orgasm slammed into her, stealing her breath. A spasm rocked her while bursts of electricity caused her channel to pulse and her cunt to milk his cock. Burying her face against his throat, she muffled the whimpering she couldn't choke down.

The fog of lust suffocating her receded, allowing reality to seep in. "Holy shit. Kerry will tell everyone." At her horrified whisper, a rumble of laughter slipped from Knox, causing his chest to vibrate. She pinched his side and he shook even harder before a snort escaped. It was sort of funny, but she'd be damned if she let him know it. Of course, nothing could dampen the swell of happiness inside her, not even the knowledge that she would soon have to make the walk of shame from the club.

Chapter Five

November

Dane completed sixteen weeks of in-patient rehab, revealing a dedication to recovery he'd never shown in the past. Rhys felt sure this miracle would not have occurred if not for the incident with Mandy. Not that Rhys was grateful Dane had hurt her. However, he did hope this was the first step toward fixing everything broken, beginning with his family. Of course, it would help if he could find Knox. He'd stopped by his house several times, but Knox was never there. No one had seen him at No Rival. The only place he'd not checked was Grid Iron.

When Rhys spotted the gorgeous woman working the front desk of the Grid Iron club, he stole a moment to watch her.

She was easily a foot shorter than he was and her sleek brown locks framed her sharply angled face to perfection. Her curves were made for a man's enjoyment. The things he could do with someone like her. He shook off the thought.

Donning his most charming smile, he strode confidently toward the entrance as if he belonged. Rhys tossed a heavy wink her way as he passed by. "I'm going to pop in and snag my brother. I'll only be a minute."

To his surprise, her brow furrowed and she moved faster than any woman he'd ever seen in his life. Stepping into his path, she forced him to draw up short of his goal. "Excuse me, sir. You're not allowed past this point unless you're a member."

"I'm just here to see my brother, Knox Collier. I'm not interested in doing anything else." He added a hot glance down the length of her body to let her know he wasn't opposed to being convinced to try a few things. It was a mistake.

Her nostrils flared and something dark flashed in her eyes. "No membership, no entry."

The brunette blocked his way as sure as if she was twice his size instead of half. He fell back on his natural charm and lowered his voice to the one used every time he was going in for the kill. "Look..." He trailed off hoping she would supply her name, and when she didn't, he lost an ounce of confidence. "My brother is here almost every day. If you'll, at the very least, let me know if he's here today, then I'll be out of your hair. It's not like I'm trying to break in and work out for free or anything." He snapped his teeth together when he realized he was on the verge of sounding idiotic.

"As I said, only members are allowed past this point, and their privacy is one of our top priorities."

Her expression never changed, and something about her struck him as familiar. He recognized that poker face. "Do you know Ryan Crawford?" Nothing. Not even a blink.

"If you're interested in signing up for Mr. Crawford's self-defense class, you can find the form online at our website."

Damn, she was a tough one. "Can I leave a note for Knox?"

"Rhys?"

The sound of his name caused him to turn. Ryan hovered in the entryway, eyeing him curiously. Obviously believing Ryan had things under control, the brown-haired girl dipped back behind the counter. "Thank goodness, a friendly face," Rhys called out in relief. "I was beginning to think the club's guard dog would have me arrested for trying to see my brother." He waved a hand toward the girl at the sign-in desk in case Ryan hadn't understood who he meant.

Ryan's eyes lit with humor and the brunette snorted, showing the first sign of life since his arrival. "I'm just coming in for the day, so I'm not sure if Knox is here. If you'll give me a minute, I'll run inside and check."

"Thank you. I'd appreciate that. I haven't been able to get ahold of him."

Ryan glanced away uncomfortably, setting off alarm bells in his head. Something was up with Knox, and it seemed Rhys was the only person who didn't know what it was. "Kerry, try not to hurt him before I get back."

Falling back on humor, Rhys scoffed at the words. "What about after you return?" Ryan smirked as he brushed past him and headed inside. At the last moment, he paused. "You did call my sister a dog, so it's only fair she be allowed to do some damage."

Rhys groaned and the sound of Ryan's laughter rang in his ears even after he was gone. Casting a nervous glance around the room, Rhys searched for anything to concentrate on to avoid another confrontation. Apparently, he'd pissed off the universe and karma was a woman, because they were all turning on him. The white walls and black floor combination of the club's foyer felt like a holding cell. Rhys hated it. Thankfully, a glossy eight-by-ten photo hanging on the nearby wall caught Rhys' attention, giving him something to focus on. It was an image of his brother facing off against Max. Their fierce expressions captured the emotion of battle to perfection, but that wasn't what caused his heart to skip a beat. Mandy's watermark adorned the bottom right-hand corner.

"I can't believe it."

"Yeah, Mandy Everette is an awesome photographer," Kerry said behind him, making him realize he'd spoken aloud.

His chest tightened. Without turning, he muttered, "It is amazing."

"If you sign up for Ryan's class then you can see the full collection."

Her smartass comment made his eye twitch. "I'm over here minding my own business. Why do you keep busting my balls?"

"I don't like you."

"You don't know me," Rhys said

without bothering to look at her.

"I don't need to. It's obvious you have chocolate dick syndrome."

That got his attention. "What?"

She waved her hands wildly. "You know, it's when you think your dick is like chocolate. Therefore, all women should be happily sucking it, but just like with any sugary treat, you leave them empty and hating themselves afterward."

"Wow! Some man must have really done a number on you to leave you so bitter."

To his surprise, Kerry smiled sweetly. "Of course the problem must be mine. There couldn't possibly be a thing wrong with you. You're perfect, right? You smile and wink at all the girls. You give them what they want if they pout prettily enough. How could a woman go wrong?"

He ignored the niggling voice in the

back of his mind whispering she was right. "Oh. I see. You have me all figured out. There's no chance you might be wrong about me?"

Kerry eyed him closely as if seriously considering his question before answering, "Nope, not a chance. You're an empty shell."

He opened his mouth prepared to blast her but Ryan reappeared, saving her from his wrath. "He's not here." Ryan froze and looked them both over. "Is everything okay out here?"

Rhys narrowed his eyes at Kerry, silently promising retribution before turning away. "I appreciate the help. I guess I'll have to wait on him to resurface because I'm out of ideas."

"You should check with Mandy," Ryan suggested.

Rhys clasped his hands behind his

back. His knuckles cracked as he curled his fingers into a fist. "Why would Mandy know where Knox is?" His voice remained steady but he couldn't hide the frost in his tone.

Luckily, Ryan didn't appear to notice. "I assumed they were inseparable," he answered with a shrug. "You never see one without the other anymore."

He would kill someone. It was the only thought rattling through his brain as he thanked Ryan for his help. Even as Rhys made the fifteen-minute drive to Mandy's, he couldn't picture anything other than wrapping his fingers around Knox's throat.

A faint glow emanated around the closed blinds of Mandy's front window, and Knox's 2014 GMC Sierra sat parked next to her car. Rhys spent several minutes staring at the window attempting to see any hint of life coming from inside. He had to know. When he could no longer stand the curiosity, he threw open the door on his truck, still unsure of how to approach this. If he beat on the door and openly accused Knox of moving in on his woman, Mandy would never forgive him if it turned out his suspicions were wrong. The pitch-black darkness outside made it easy for him to peek around the cracks of her blinds. Unfortunately, it didn't allow for much of a view. He could see the empty kitchen but nothing else. No sounds emerged from inside and the lack of activity made his skin crawl. If this were an innocent visit, there would be the sound of voices or a TV floating through the thin walls.

He didn't have high hopes her spare key would be in the same spot, and he was more than a little surprised when he found it still under the flowerpot. Moving as quietly as possible, he let himself in. Rhys braced for Mandy to blast him, but no attack came. The front room was empty. A t-shirt on the floor caught his eye as he slipped inside, making sure to latch the door behind him. The article of clothing looked suspiciously like something he'd seen Knox wear. A few feet from the shirt was a lacy bra, and Rhys followed the trail of discarded clothing through the house until the bathroom came into view. Steam rolled from the open doorway, and the splash of water seemed unnaturally loud in the otherwise silent house.

The thick carpet of the hallway muffled his footfalls as he moved closer. A gap in the shower curtain gave him a clear view of Mandy against the wall. Water dripped from her blonde locks and rolled down her face. Her eyes were closed as she panted for breath. A flush covered her pale skin and a strangled cry left her throat as the man rocking against her brought her to release. The opaque shower curtain hid most of the man's features from view and his face was buried in the crook of Mandy's neck, but Rhys would recognize his brother anywhere. Time lost all meaning as he watched them together. It could have been seconds or an hour passing him by.

When the feeling returned to his limbs, he took a step backward and then another until he was standing at the door of his truck with no memory of how he came to be there. Knox and Mandy. Everything hurt. A sharp pain pierced him between the eyes and his chest felt tight. He couldn't leave. Without any real plan in mind, he sat behind the wheel and stared at her apartment until he felt sure they should be able to feel his gaze penetrating the walls. He didn't have many people he cared about, but two of them were inside...together. How could they betray him like this?

A huge part of Rhys wanted to go back inside and drag Knox from the shower. The rest of him was just numb. He forced his mind to go blank and he sat back to wait. Knox would have to leave sometime and he would be here. After all, it was a fight night. What felt like an eternity later, Knox appeared in the doorway, blocking out the light streaming from inside with his large frame. He took a couple steps before spinning and hauling Mandy out with him. Her laughter rang through the parking lot before Knox cut off the sound by covering her mouth with his own.

The rage finally came and Rhys

slipped from the vehicle once more. He wove his way through the other cars parked in the lot, staying out of sight. A groan only a doomed man could make escaped Knox as he pulled away from Mandy. "It's cold. What are you doing outside with no clothes on?" he asked as he attempted to push her back inside. Rhys had never seen his brother playful with anyone before. It made him seem even more of a stranger. Unguarded, Knox appeared younger and Rhys couldn't look away from his face. He hid in the shadows, watching until Knox was backing out of his spot. Mandy leaned against the doorframe until his truck was out of sight, and as she took a step backward into the house, Rhys made his move.

* * * * *

The hot water pounding on his back while his cock pumped inside Mandy's tight heat was a sensation Knox could not shake. He couldn't get enough of her. With his eyes locked on the road in front of him, he tried to shove her into a box inside his mind, but Mandy refused to budge. She was always right there taunting him with his need. Damn, he wanted to turn around and go back. Even after she'd coated his body with soap, he still swore he could smell her on his skin.

His needy cock twitched to life and a rumble of laughter escaped him. By all accounts, his dick should be dead. The picture of Mandy taking him between her lips flashed across his mind. He was so fucked. One day he would wake up and simply refuse to leave their bed. Damn, he was near to there now. Touching his lips, Knox physically attempted to wipe away his smile. No matter how he tried, it snapped back into place. At some point in the past few months, the echo of Mandy's voice inside his head had become louder than the demons haunting him. The time had come for him to talk to Rhys. He'd put it off too long as it was. They never spent more than half an hour in each other's company, so it hadn't been hard to avoid the subject of Mandy. The reasons for his silence were purely selfish. He knew Rhys would be pissed and he wasn't ready to have his peace disrupted. Tonight Knox had ensured the topic could no longer be avoided. Even the thought of Rhys' anger could not dispel his happiness. The picture of Mandy's expression as he'd dropped to one knee would not leave his mind. She'd been ecstatic. How had he gotten so lucky? Mandy shouldn't have looked at him twice. Now not only was she going to marry him, she was overjoyed at the prospect.

Fuck it. Knox whipped a U-turn. He was going home. There would be time for a thousand matches, but tonight, he wanted to be with Mandy, and kissing her feet for taking a chance on him.

* * * * *

"Is this some attempt to get even with me?"

Mandy gasped in surprise when Rhys spoke, seeming to appear out of nowhere.

"If so, then let me know when you're finished because I want my life back. I want you back."

She clutched at her chest attempting to slow the racing of her heart. She hated when people snuck up on her. Four months. He had been gone from her life for sixteen whole weeks, and at the first sight of him, she made an unfortunate discovery. She was still pissed.

"Of all the egotistical—" She broke

off and counted to ten in her head. "To hell with this," she muttered, turning away and heading inside. She intended to leave him standing on the sidewalk, but he stormed in behind her as if he belonged there.

He snagged her arm, halting her progress. "How is it egotistical? We were happy before you threw me out of your life."

She didn't know him. Most likely, she never really had. Perhaps he'd charmed her, or she'd built him up in her mind. Either way, she didn't know the person standing in front of her. "Happy," she repeated, unable to believe her ears. "What fucking planet do you live on? I've been happier these past few months than I have ever been in my life and it has nothing to do with you."

"Damn it, Mandy. He is broken.

Knox is my brother and I love him, but he is damaged."

Inexplicably, she found herself smiling. "Just like me." Her smile fell, and she shook her head before adding, "Better a broken man than someone who breaks me."

Rhys snorted. "Then you're an idiot because I would have given you everything. But you'll end up with nothing because Knox won't be happy until he's dead. You can't fix him."

A burst of anger shot through her. "He's a hell of a lot stronger than you give him credit for."

The smirk on Rhys' face made her hand itch to slap him. "Where do you think he is right now?"

"He has a fight scheduled," she answered immediately, and his smug look slipped a bit before falling back into place.

She knew Rhys thought Knox would not have told her.

"Why didn't he take you with him, then?"

Mandy rolled her eyes. "Some of us have to work for a living, Rhys. I can't spend my nights on the town and roll into my place of business at the crack of dawn, half-asleep."

"And that's another conversation we will be having soon as well, since you should be in school. For now, though, I want to know if he offered to take you with him."

"No," she admitted before adding, "nor did I ask him to, and my education is none of your business. Knox knows how important this new job is to me. He wouldn't do anything to risk it."

"New job?" Rhys repeated, sounding dumbfounded.

"Yes, Rhys. New job. I swear. You never, ever know what's going on."

"Oh. I know that shit is right. Just like I didn't know you were pregnant with my baby."

If he thought to catch her unawares by hoping Knox had not confessed to telling him about the baby, then he was mistaken. She would never give him the satisfaction, even if he possessed the ability. "Why are you so convinced he's hiding something from me?"

"Because he doesn't want this."

Anger over his low blow caused her to eye to twitch. "It sure felt to me like he wanted everything we've done."

Rhys growled at her open taunt. "Not you. There is not a man in his right mind who wouldn't want you. I meant this," he said, throwing his arms wide. "He doesn't want life in general. It is—I don't know, lacking or some shit. He will not stop what he is doing until he is dead, and I'm having a hard fucking time accepting what I'm seeing with my own damn eyes. He won't quit even for you."

"I didn't ask him to, Rhys. I didn't fall in love with what I thought I could make him into." The declaration hung in the air between them. Rhys looked as if she'd punched him in the gut, but she wouldn't take it back. "I love Knox because of who he already is. Broken. Hard. I love it all."

The loud chirp of his phone interrupted her rant. "Fuck!" Rhys swore as he ripped the phone from his pocket. "This is not the goddamn time." His face went pale. "What? When?" The look on his face scared the hell out of her.

Without offering a goodbye, Rhys crammed the phone back into his pocket.

"Let's go," he said snagging her arm and dragging her along in his wake.

"Wait. What's going on? I don't have any shoes on and my hair is wet."

With a frustrated curse, Rhys turned on her. "Get your shoes on and get in the fucking truck, Mandy. A cement rig sideswiped Knox's truck not even two miles from here. If we leave now, we might beat the ambulance to the hospital."

The room spun but nothing could have gotten her feet moving faster.

Chapter Six

A silent truce fell between the three of them during the four days they sat at Knox's bedside. Unfortunately, the more time passed without Knox waking up, the angrier Rhys became. The left side of Knox's body was a mess of bruising, open cuts and scratches. Miraculously, he'd somehow managed to avoid any broken bones. It didn't matter. With the steering wheel pushed against his chest cutting off the oxygen to his brain, Knox had fallen into a comatose state they didn't know if he'd recover from. The swelling had receded but Knox's condition had not improved.

In harsh contrast to Knox's battered state, Dane appeared healthier than ever, if not a bit subdued even for him. He'd gained some of his weight back. The sharp cheekbones, which Rhys had grown accustomed to seeing in the past year, were almost gone. His blond hair had also regained some life. He turned a book over several times between his hands. Rhys had given up trying to see the title over an hour ago.

Switching his attention to Mandy, he spent a few minutes watching her. She looked tired. With her forehead resting on her crossed arms on the bed at Knox's hip, she almost appeared to be sleeping. He knew better. She hadn't slept a wink since they'd gotten the news. None of them had. For some reason, one he could not explain, the knowledge pissed him off even more. It would be just like Knox to bail when they needed him the most.

"I told you you'd get hurt," he lashed

out before he could stop himself. She answered without opening her eyes, proving he had been right about her not sleeping.

"No. I'm not."

He snorted. "So, you won't shed a single tear when he dies?"

At his question, Dane stood and left the room. Mandy finally lifted her chin to look at him. "He won't die."

His throat swelled at the conviction in her blue eyes. Pain had forced him to say the words hoping to hurt her, but he needed her reassurance. "How do you know?" His question came out sounding as ravaged as he felt.

Mandy brushed her fingers over Knox's scarred knuckles. "Because he promised I would never hurt again, and I trust him."

"Realized something." The sound of Knox's voice startled Rhys and his eyes shot to his brother's face. Knox's were still closed, but Mandy covered her mouth as if holding back sobs. The move proved he had not been hearing things.

Mandy brushed a tear away before asking, "What did you realize, baby?"

"Don't want to die."

"Oh sweetie. I knew that."

He didn't say anything else, and Mandy dropped her chin to her arm on the bed, but she kept her face turned toward Knox. His eyes still didn't open, but he moved his hand until it rested against her cheek. "Was joke. Supposed to laugh," he slurred after a minute.

Mandy's breathing shuddered. "I'm laughing on the inside."

"Don't cry," Knox whispered, sounding tired. "Love you. Would never leave you." A noise almost like a hiccup escaped Mandy. "I love you too much to let you go."

Rhys stood. "I'll find a nurse or something," he offered. At his offer, Knox turned his head in his direction. "My brother is here?" One green eye peeked open before falling closed again. "Looks like shit."

Rhys snorted at the assessment. "Yeah, well, you're not looking too swift yourself, buddy."

"Dane?"

"I'm here," Dane said from the doorway, startling Rhys with his reappearance. "You good?"

At Knox's question, Dane's mouth turned up in one corner. "Yeah. I'm solid."

"Good," Knox said, his tone a bit stronger than before. "Touch Mandy again and I will kill you."

Even half-dead, Rhys didn't doubt the truth in Knox's promise, but Dane's smile grew. "I wouldn't expect anything less."

"Love you guys," Knox said raggedly. "Now go away. You're tired and Mandy is crying."

Dane straightened away from the doorframe. "Sure, man. Call if you need anything and I'll be around." Without waiting for a response, he ducked back out of the room. Rhys knew he should go as well, but he couldn't force his feet to move. In a short few minutes, Knox had gone from a four-day coma to lecturing them and scooting over in his bed to make room for Mandy. "I need to hold you." The desperate note behind Knox's statement had Mandy climbing into his arms. As soon as she settled against Knox's side, his breathing became steadier. "I'm having your shit moved to my house," he whispered against her hair. "I cannot stand a single moment of being without you."

The way he held Mandy and spoke to her was private. There was an intimacy between them Rhys wasn't meant to play witness to, but he couldn't look away. Rhys' eyes stung. He had done everything wrong while the brother he'd always thought of as irredeemable had sat by, quietly loving her. Rhys didn't deserve her.

Moving silently from the room, Rhys made it as far as the wall outside the door before his legs wouldn't carry him any farther. With his back pressed against the cool plaster, he sank to the floor. Space and time, those were the things he'd given Mandy in the hopes she would find her way back to him. At least, he'd told himself as much. It was a lie, of course. Feeding on self-deception to get through the day had become almost second nature. Truth meant acceptance. Acceptance meant a thousand complications he wasn't prepared to face.

Shying away from the dark pathways in his mind, Rhys turned his head to watch Dane sitting against the opposite wall a few doors down. He'd become so lost to his own demons, he had not realized Dane was there or that he wasn't alone. Kerry sat at his side with her legs crossed and feet tucked beneath her thighs. A huge bouquet of flowers rested on the floor beside her and she flipped through the pages of Dane's book. With their heads close together, the pair laughed at something inside. Comprehension descended upon Rhys. He was the one with the walls. Knox and Dane weren't the ones who were broken. He was. In spite of all the pain, they still let people in. Rhys didn't.

As if feeling his stare, they both looked his way at the same time. Dane eyed him carefully, making Rhys wonder what he saw. Kerry's laughter immediately fled at the sight of him. A few quiet words passed between the pair and Dane rose to his feet before helping Kerry to hers. She brushed the dust from the seat of her dark jeans before sweeping the flowers from the floor. Dane attempted to play the gentleman by relieving her of the burden, but she waved his hands away. Rhys almost laughed at her inability to let a man do anything for her. No doubt she owned a collection of vibrators in different shapes and sizes, serving every purpose, including allowing her complete control.

Rhys didn't trouble himself to stand when they moved to his side. Tilting his chin back, he met her green eyes without bothering to hide his animosity. "I see you've met my brother Dane." Even he was taken by surprise by the dislike in his voice. As far as he was aware, he'd never openly hated anyone. It seemed Kerry was the exception.

If she was bothered by the fact in any way, she didn't show it. "Oh, I've known Dane for a while. Him, I like," she added, and if he wasn't mistaken a glimmer of defiance lit her gaze. Dane released a low chuckle. It was obvious his brother thought she was joking, and Kerry dared Rhys with her eyes to call her on it. Challenge accepted.

"I am beyond curious as to why you hated me on sight? Most people find me a complete delight." Rhys added a wink, intent on goading her. When her spine stiffened, he knew he'd hit his mark. Dane looked back and forth between them as if working out a puzzle, but Rhys kept his concentration locked on Kerry. She made him forget what he'd lost. Mandy. Damn, he'd lost everything. Her methodology was rage invoking, but it worked.

"Most people have never gotten a good look at a certain five-page-long bill." The air left his lungs. She knew. She'd always known. Some of what he was feeling must have shown in his expression. For the first time ever in his presence, she shifted nervously. A roar buzzed in his ears, but it still couldn't shut out the sound of her voice when she spoke again. "The guys at Grid Iron sent me over to deliver these to Mandy." She nodded at the bouquet in her hands. "They figure Knox would laugh at flowers but Mandy could use the cheering up." She was rambling. Another first. Her jaw visibly tightened, making Rhys wonder if she'd come to the same conclusion. His chest burned and fire licked at the back of his throat. Unable to stand anything more, he dropped his gaze to the tile floor.

He couldn't think of a single thing to say. It didn't matter anyhow. She would never understand. The baby Mandy lost was his loss as well. Kerry ground out a curse before sighing heavily. "I've changed my mind. Dane, do you mind taking these flowers inside?"

As soon as they were alone, Kerry sank to her knees in front of him and sat back on her heels. She waited until he met her stare before speaking again. "Air, food and water," she said, causing his brow to furrow in confusion. When he didn't ask what she meant, she sighed again. "Those are the three things people require to survive," she explained. "If you have those, you can get up every morning and continue existing. People need love and acceptance to thrive. The thing is, you also have to be willing to love and accept others." She glanced away but it was too late. He'd seen a flash of pain inside her before she'd hidden it from him. Every word she said was the truth, but he couldn't understand why she said them at all. "For what it's worth, I don't really think you're an empty shell," she added, taking him by surprise.

"Why are you telling me this?"

"Because I don't hate you. I don't even know you, but I do know Knox. I've known him for several years. He is completely incapable of charming his way into anyone's life. He's socially inept. All he's ever done is exist. Then one day he introduced me to this beautiful broken woman, and for the first time ever, I witnessed a miracle. I saw him thrive. It was immediately apparent she didn't see the merciless man the rest of the world does when they look at Knox, and the way he watches her..." She shook her head as if she couldn't explain it. "It's almost enough to restore someone's faith. Not mine, of course, but truly what they have is a rare light in an otherwise ugly world."

The combination of no sleep and watching his dreams slip away left Rhys in a numb haze. It was the only explanation he could conjure for his complete inability to comprehend the point in her reasoning. "I guess I'm especially dense today because I still don't get why you're telling me this."

Kerry shrugged helplessly. "You have it all," she explained, sounding exasperated. "You're charming, sexy and no doubt you're nice to the elderly. I wouldn't be surprised to learn you can cause women to orgasm without ever touching them. I mean really. It's not fair." He tried hard not to smirk, but the temptation was too much. He was fairly certain she would hit him. Thankfully, she only rolled her eyes before adding, "I'm not complimenting you. You must have made Mandy's life hell, because you do not love her, and she totally deserves someone who does."

He sort of wished she had hit him. It would have hurt less. "I do too." Even to his ears, he sounded childish, but he did love Mandy.

Kerry looked angry again. "Please. Spare me. You fuck every woman you see with your eyes. Men who are in love don't do that."

"Ha!" Rhys shouted before she could say another word. "You obviously don't know shit about men. Even if they're married to the world's sexiest supermodel they still look at every other woman."

"Maybe so, but they don't roll out

the welcome mat with their gaze," she shot back. There's a difference between looking and—" She broke off and growled. "Never mind. One of these days, you'll meet someone and you'll realize you never loved Mandy. If you loved her, I mean really loved her—not just felt as if she's a friend you couldn't live without—you would have staked your claim and refused to budge. You would have fought to the death to keep her and killed Knox for even thinking of touching her. You sure as hell would have been there when she needed you the most." She ran a shaking hand through her hair and stood. He wanted to scream at her and deny every word she said, but he couldn't think of a single argument. Why hadn't he done those things? "Look, I have shit to do today and I didn't come here to fight with you. Have a nice life."

Without a backward glance, she sailed inside Knox's room, leaving Rhys to his anger and with no outlet in sight. Unable to stand another moment inside his own skin, he went in search of the nearest exit. Maybe one day he'd agree with everything Kerry said, but today wasn't that day.

* * * * *

The hospital released Knox after only one night of observation and a barrage of tests. Mandy could have sworn she heard a cheer erupt as they pulled out of the parking lot. She'd never seen a worse patient. Two hours after he'd awaken, she'd given up trying to smooth things over with the nurses. She recognized the futility of her actions the moment Knox dared them to attempt to stop him from walking out of the building if they made her leave the room for any reason.

Staying true to his word of moving

her in with him, all her things were transferred to his house before the end of the night. Kerry proved her efficiency by handling everything, including finding someone to sublet her apartment. The moment Knox walked through the door of what was now their home, his whole body seemed to relax as he stared at the sight of her things alongside his. A sheepish smile touched his lips. "I'm sorry."

"For what?"

"Being me," he answered with a shrug.

Not until that moment did she realize he'd been trapped behind his walls with so many people around. She no longer lived on the outside of his cold shell and couldn't see what other people did. The knowledge made her eyes sting.

"You're perfect as you are. Never be sorry."

Tossing aside the bag she'd packed for him but he wouldn't let her carry, Knox shrugged off his coat and kicked off his shoes. Mandy kept one eye locked on him while doing the same. She kept expecting him to disappear. The second she finished hanging her coat up, he snagged the back of her neck and lowered his mouth to hers. At the first brush of his soft lips, her heart squeezed in her chest. She'd been so close to losing him. The fear she'd stamped down came rushing to the surface and she could barely breathe. Her throat swelled. The desire to climb him like a tree and re-fuse to allow him out of her sight again crippled her. She didn't know where to put her hands.

He leaned away and a line appeared between his brows. "Did I do something wrong?"

She shook her head, barely able to

speak past the lump in her throat. "I'm scared of hurting you. You're too stubborn to tell me if I am." The world tilted and the floor disappeared beneath her feet before she could blink. She struggled against his hold as he carried her to the bedroom. "See? You're going to hurt yourself."

"Stay still. You're hurting me now."

She immediately went limp. He flashed an incredulous look her way. "I can't believe you fell for that." With a growl, she attempted to slide out of his grip but he dropped her on the bed and covered her body with his before she could get away. "Seriously, Mandy, give a man a break."

Hearing the pain in his voice, she quit struggling. "I almost lost you." Saying the words aloud broke something free and she had to gasp to pull oxygen into her lungs. Knox brushed her hair away from her face and held her gaze until the darkness left the corners of her vision.

"I need you calm because I have some things I need to say." Simply hearing him say he needed her caused her body to relax. "The first time I made love to you I had three broken ribs."

She'd never broken any bones but she was given to understand it hurt.

"Why didn't you say anything?" Huh. She sounded reasonable. Maybe she should take up acting.

"When you're touching me, I don't feel anything else." He was sweet but she was still aggravated. It fled when he continued. "I love you. More than that, I am incomplete without you. This house is paid for, along with everything else I own. There's also close to four hundred and fifty thousand dollars in my checking account."

Her brain blacked out even though she was clearly still conscious. "Okay," she said, unable to think of a thing to fill the void. His monetary worth meant nothing to her. "Would you like me to sign a pre-nup?"

He looked incredulous for a moment. "Are you fucking kidding me? No. My point is the exact opposite. I need to know you're taken care of. I mean, those bastards at the hospital tried to make you leave my room because of a piece of paper. What if I had died?" A muscle in his jaw twitched and she could practically hear him counting to ten in his head before he could continue. "The thing is, I want to do the big wedding thing. I know it's odd for a guy, but it's like I want show the world you're mine. Here's the problem. With all the planning and time that goes into a full wedding, I also want to marry you now."

She couldn't love him more. "I only want to be with you. Whatever you decide is fine with me."

"I want both," he admitted. "I want to get married now and do the big wedding later. I know you don't care about the money, and really I don't either, but it is years of fifty-two weekends a year of my blood. Every drop of my blood belongs to you."

She could see how important her answer was to him by the set lines of his face. He wouldn't relax until she agreed. "Are you sure?"

A smile lingered on his lips but refused to break free. "Are you saying yes?"

Six months earlier, she would have never pictured this moment. With a short nod, she sealed her fate. "Will you at least take a nap first?"

His mouth turned up in one corner

and a wicked glint touched his eyes. Shifting positions, he made sure she couldn't miss the erection pressed between them. "Naps are for pussies."

The End

Keep an eye out for book 3, Unequaled

Author Bio

Charity Parkerson is an award winning and multi-published author with several companies. Born with no filter from her brain to her mouth, she decided to take this odd quirk and insert it in her characters.

*2015 Readers' Favorite Award Winner
*Winner of 2, 2014 Readers' Favorite Awards
*2015 Passionate Plume Award Finalist
*2013 Readers' Favorite Award Winner
*2013 Reviewers' Choice Award Winner
*2012 ARRA Finalist for Favorite Paranormal Romance
*Five-time winner of The Mistress of the Darkpath

Connect with her online:

--Website: charityparkerson.com

--Facebook: facebook.com/authorCharityParkerson

facebook.com/TheMenofSin

--Twitter: twitter.com/CharityParkerso